# ALL
# THE MONEY
# IN THE
# WORLD

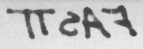

# ALL THE MONEY IN THE WORLD

## by Bill Brittain

**Illustrations by Charles Robinson**

HarperTrophy
*A Division of* HarperCollins*Publishers*

ALL THE MONEY IN THE WORLD

Library of Congress Cataloging-in-Publication Data
Brittain, Bill.
  All the money in the world.

  Summary: When Quentin gets his wish for all the money in the world, he gets a pack of troubles too.
  [1. Money—Fiction]   I. Robinson, Charles,
1931–    II. Title.
PZ7.B78067A1      [Fic]       77-25635
ISBN 0-06-020675-6
ISBN 0-06-020676-4 (lib. bdg.)
ISBN 0-06-440128-6 (pbk.)

First Harper Trophy edition, 1982.


*Manufactured in the United Kingdom by* HarperCollins

*For Ginnie*

# Contents

# 1
# Big Dreams . . . Big Fish

"Nothing's biting today except little ones. See?"

Something wriggly and wet landed in Quentin Stowe's lap. At the same time he heard a shrill laugh from Roselynn Peabody, standing beside him at the edge of the pond.

Quentin's eyes popped open. In the cool shade of the big rock, he'd almost fallen asleep. For a moment he just gazed at the tiny yellow-and-green perch that Roselynn had dropped on him. Then he smiled lazily, scooped it up, and tossed it back into the water.

"There's bigger fish in here," he said. "Eating-sized bass. If we wait long enough, one of 'em is bound to bite."

"Then let's get busy and catch one." Farther down the bank Vincent Arbor flicked his wrist, and his shiny new fishing pole snapped the glittering lure almost all the way across the pond. It hit the water with a tiny splash, and he began reeling in the line.

"If I had a pole like yours or Vincent's I'd show you how to catch fish, all right," Quentin said to Roselynn.

Roselynn and Vincent had whippy steel poles with reels that made casting bait about as easy as throwing a stone. Quentin's pole was just a branch cut from a willow tree with the twigs lopped off. He'd twisted a piece of thin wire to the end of it for a line, and his bait was a hookful of worms he'd dug up back at the farm.

"Want to use my pole?" Roselynn held it out to him. "I don't mind."

Quentin shook his head. Roselynn was a real friend. She'd let him ride her new bike or borrow her baseball glove for important games—things like that. But borrowing was different from owning. You always had to give borrowed things back. He dreamed of having a pole of his own, to use any time he wanted to.

He leaned back against the cool rock and closed his eyes again. In his mind he could still see the green-and-yellow fish that had landed in his lap.

Colors—funny thing about colors. The fish had green-and-yellow skin. Roselynn had white skin—

2

"But Poppa? For years he worked for other men. He picked beans and tomatoes and cucumbers and whatever needed harvesting. He'd come home nights with his back hurting so much he couldn't stand straight.

"But he saved his money. Not like some of that no-account trash he worked with. And one day he had enough to buy this farm.

"Poppa would like to buy things for you, Quentin. But most of our money has to go toward paying off what we owe the bank. One day, though, we'll be free and clear, and then every penny Poppa earns from this farm will be ours. Won't that be something?"

Quentin agreed that would be something. And he made up his mind he'd never again tell Poppa and Momma about his dreams.

But sometimes—like right now—he couldn't help dreaming about getting something not because he *needed* it, but just because he *wanted* it.

"Vincent?" he said slowly, opening his eyes.

"Yeah, Quent?"

"Do you have one thing you dream about? More than anything else in the world?"

Vincent thought about this for a minute. "Yeah," he said finally.

"What is it?" asked Roselynn. "Come on, Vincent."

"More than anything else, I want to be a deputy

sheriff. A Cedar Ferry policeman like my father."

"I bet you'll do it too," said Roselynn. "When you're older."

"But I can't wait," Vincent replied. "I want it now."

"You haven't even finished school yet," said Quentin, shaking his head.

Vincent stood up straight and crossed his arms. "I'll bet they'd make me a deputy anyway, if I could find out what went on in town last night. Dad was out three times in the police car."

Quentin leaned forward. "What do you mean?" he asked. "What went on?"

"The first thing was at Mrs. Trussker's house. She was practicing her singing when she suddenly let out a yell like a steam whistle. Dad went over to see what the trouble was. Wow, the story she told him!"

"What kind of a story?" Quentin asked.

"She said she saw a man looking in at her window. And the man's face was *green*!"

"Green?" Quentin snorted. "She probably just got dizzy from singing so loud. In the church choir she sounds like a cat with its tail caught in the door."

"My daddy says it's more like a screech owl with a sore toe." Roselynn giggled.

"Well that's not all," Vincent went on. "Old Mr.

Barclay couldn't sleep because of a toothache. He was out on his porch in his rocking chair. He saw something run across the front lawn. At first he thought it was a dog or a cat. But whoever heard of a dog or a cat wearing a top hat and holding a pipe in its mouth?"

"Mr. Barclay was seeing things," said Quentin doubtfully. "Maybe because of the toothache?"

Vincent shrugged. "All I know is, a lot of people heard the awful sound a few minutes later."

"Sound? What sound?"

"It was loud and scary," said Vincent. "Nobody knew what it was. Then Dad talked to Mr. Herricks. He's traveled all over the world. Mr. Herricks said he'd only heard it once before. In India." Vincent looked from Quentin to Roselynn. "He said it was the roar a tiger makes just before it leaps on its prey!"

"Wow!" breathed Roselynn. "If you could find out about all those things, they'd *have* to make you a cop. Right away."

"Anyway, being a deputy sheriff's my best dream." Vincent turned to Roselynn. "What's yours?"

"I don't know. My dreams keep changing. Sometimes I want to act in the movies. Or maybe win a gold medal in the Olympic games. And I'd really like to have my own color TV, and . . ."

"Okay, okay," Vincent said with a grin. "One thing at a time. How about you, Quentin? What's your special dream?"

"Right now it's catching a really big fish. But I'm like Roselynn, I guess. There are so many . . ."

*Tap . . . tap, tap . . . TAP . . .*

The end of Quentin's fishing pole jerked up and down several times. Then it bent into a big curve. Quentin yanked up hard on the pole. Whatever was on the other end of the line pulled down just as hard.

"It's a fish!" shouted Vincent. "A big one. Don't pull too hard or you'll break the line."

"Line . . . won't break," Quentin puffed. "It's . . . made . . . of wire." Gripping the pole tightly, he stood up and peered down into the water.

"Lucky it bit on *your* hook," said Roselynn. "He'd have snapped my line on the first run."

Quentin opened his mouth to answer. But just then the fish pulled mightily at the line. Quentin felt himself yanked forward. He put out a foot to get his balance.

But when he put his foot down, there wasn't any ground beneath it. His whole body leaned out over the water.

*SPLASH!*

The water closed over Quentin's head and pushed into his nose and mouth. He swam back to

8

the surface, sneezing and coughing. When he was finally able to open his eyes he saw his pole being pulled to the far end of the pond.

"Come on, Quentin!" shouted Roselynn. "The fish is still hooked. Go get the pole."

Quentin grabbed Vincent's hand and scrambled up the bank. As he ran along the shore, water streamed from his clothes.

He caught up with the pole at the far end of the pond. He pulled the line, expecting that the fish had escaped.

The fish pulled back. But not as hard this time. It was getting tired.

Quentin backed toward a place where the shore was flat and muddy. There he waited, always keeping a steady pull on the line.

Suddenly the water shot upward in sprays of little drops. It was almost as if a bomb had gone off on the pond's bottom. At the same time the biggest fish Quentin had ever seen leaped into the air. It skittered along the surface on its tail for several feet and then plopped back into the water.

Quentin moved back to the grassy part of the bank. Slowly he pulled the pole upward.

"There he is!" shouted Roselynn. "Look."

At first it looked like a big rock being towed through the shallows. Then it turned on its side, and they could see the white belly of the fish.

"It's really big!" screamed Vincent.

Quentin kept moving backward until at last the fish lay on the grassy bank, flopping about helplessly.

Quentin knelt down to remove the hook. "It's a bass," he said proudly. "I guess I'd better take it right home, so Momma can get it ready for supper."

"And I'm going to get me a willow branch and a piece of wire to make a pole like yours," said Vincent with a smile. "Maybe next time my folks can have fish for supper, too."

Quentin put the fish in the basket of his bicycle. "See you tomorrow?" he asked.

"Sure," Roselynn answered. "Where'll we meet?"

"At my house," said Quentin. "Come after lunch. I'll have my chores done by then."

He got on his bike and pedaled up the dirt path toward the road.

Well, I got the biggest fish, he thought. Just the way I wished I would. But wishing and dreaming could go on forever. There were lots of things Quentin wanted. A new fishing rod, a baseball glove. Or something for Momma or Poppa. A new coat for Momma, maybe, or a tractor for Poppa that really ran right. Or maybe . . .

Before he'd pedaled the first mile, Quentin was

wishing for a brand-new ten-speed bike like Rose-lynn's. His own rusty bicycle had a broken pedal, and his front wheel wasn't quite round. It's funny, he thought, I always feel like I'm pedaling uphill.

He came to the old abandoned schoolhouse. It had big holes in the roof, and a flock of pigeons was nesting in the bell tower. He gave the pigeons a friendly wave.

*Psssssssss*

The front wheel of the bike wobbled slightly. Quentin felt as if he were pedaling through deep mud.

Flat tire.

He stopped and got off. The fish in his basket looked as sad and tired as Quentin felt. He tossed it onto the flattened grass of the school yard and opened the little pouch of tools behind the seat.

With a wrench he took off the front wheel and looked at the worn tire. There it was. A piece of glass.

It was hot work, patching the tube and then putting the tire back on the wheel. "Seems like there's more patches than tube," he said.

The old hand pump he kept tied to the rear carrier was rusty, and it leaked at every stroke, but it slowly filled the tire with air. By the time he'd finished, his arms ached, and the hot sun was making him sweat. But finally the tire was filled enough

12

to ride on. He climbed onto the bike.

*Pssssssssss*

Another leak? Or maybe the patch hadn't held.

For almost an hour Quentin worked on the tire. He put patches all over the tube—even over other patches. Then he pumped up the tire and got ready to ride off.

*Pssssssssss*

Angrily he kicked at the bicycle. He was going to have to walk home.

He went to get the fish. As he came near it, a swarm of flies drifted upward. He smelled something—something bad. And it wasn't hard to figure out what it was.

In the heat of the sun the fish had spoiled. Now it was a dry, smelly thing, good only to feed the flies.

Quentin wanted to cry. What had started out as a fine surprise for Momma and Poppa was ruined.

But he didn't want to leave the fish there beside the road with flies buzzing around it. It deserved better than to be a bit of roadside trash.

At the side of the school he found a spot where some boards lay flat on the ground. One of the boards was broken as if someone had dropped a rock through it. Quentin got down on his hands and knees and peered through the opening.

An abandoned well. Just the place for the fish. A

lot better than burying it where some dog might dig it up.

Quentin carried the fish to the hole and dropped it in. A moment later there was the sound of a splash as the fish hit the water below.

"Hey, you! You up there."

Startled, Quentin looked about. Had he imagined the voice? No. It had been too clear. But where . . . ?

"If you can't help me out of this beastly hole, the least you could do is stop throwing fish down on my head!"

There was someone in the well! Someone with a high, squeaky voice. Quentin knelt down, putting his face near the hole in the boards.

"Hello down there!"

"Hello yourself" was the reply. "Now are you going to help a poor old man or not?"

"How far down are you?"

"Since I'm standing up to my knees in water, I'd say I was at the bottom," said the voice. "Maybe fifteen feet down. Have you a rope or something?"

"No, I . . ." Quentin looked around. There was nothing he could use. Then he saw his fishing pole lying in the ditch.

"I have a fishing pole up here. Would that help?"

"How long is it?"

"About eight feet."

14

"Hmm." The sound echoed from the stones of the well. "Not quite enough. How strong's the line?"

"It's not line. It's wire."

"Oh, splendid. Splendid. Just lower it down to me, then."

"But the wire's not very thick."

"You'd be surprised at how little I weigh, lad. Just let it down here, and we'll make do."

Quentin got the pole and brought it to the well. He dropped the hook and the wire through. Then he put the pole into the well, tip first.

"I see it, lad," came the voice. "Just a bit further."

Quentin lay down by the hole. He held the handle end of the pole tightly and put his arm far down into the hole.

"Just a bit now. Ah, got it."

Quentin felt something jerking at the end of the line. He hoped he'd have enough strength to pull up whoever it was down there.

"Haul away, lad."

Quentin pulled up. There was nowhere near the weight at the end that he'd expected. "Are you okay?" he called.

"You're doing fine, lad. Another couple of feet and all's well."

Finally Quentin was able to grip the wire. He

continued pulling it in. He heard the voice again, quite near this time.

"That's got it, lad. And I thank you."

Something was grasping at the boards around the hole. It was a hand. But most amazing, it was a tiny hand, the hand of a doll or puppet. Yet it was alive, the little fingers clasping the wood tightly. And there was one other thing about it that made Quentin wide-eyed with wonder.

The hand was green.

# 2
# *Flan*

Silent and afraid, Quentin watched as the thing in the well pulled its way up into the sunlight.

The reaching green hand was attached to a small arm inside a sleeve of yellow-and-black-checked cloth. A battered top hat appeared as whatever it was struggled up out of the well. It muttered to itself in some strange language. Quentin couldn't make out the words, but the tone was exactly like Poppa's when he had a busy day of plowing ahead and the tractor wouldn't start.

Finally, with a gigantic *whoosh* of breath, the creature popped its head out of the well and rested for a moment, propped on its elbows.

It was a man—at least it seemed to be. But one such as Quentin had never seen before. He was no bigger than a large doll. His face, like his hands, was a pale green, seamed and wrinkled with age. His head, on which the dented top hat perched jauntily, was scarcely as big as a baseball. His eyes glittered angrily, and his teeth gnashed against the stem of a tiny pipe.

"The wet and the dark—it's more than a body should have to bear," he complained in a high, reedy voice. "Come, lad. Give us a hand. You'd not have me falling back down there, would you?"

Quentin walked to the edge of the hole. He put out his hand. The little man grasped his thumb tightly, and Quentin heaved upward. The green man came shooting out of the hole like a cork from a bottle.

For a moment he lay on the grass, gasping for breath. "It's not dignified," he wheezed. "First the singing, like the wail of the banshee. Moved me right out of house and home, it did. Then tumbling down a well and having to wait for hours. Finally a dead fish rains down on my head. Terrible way to be treated. Just terrible."

Now Quentin could hardly keep from laughing out loud. The green man, lying there in his soaked suit of yellow and black, was one of the funniest things he'd ever seen.

Finally the man got to his feet. He blew loudly into his pipe, and water spurted out of the bowl.

"How do you do?" Quentin tried to remember his manners. He put out his hand. "I'm Quentin Stowe, and you'd be . . ."

The little man looked at him strangely. "I'd be on my way, thanking you very much for pulling me out of the well." He turned about and, with a little hop-step, headed toward the road.

He hadn't gone far when the fishing pole in Quentin's hand jerked suddenly. Quentin's eyes followed the shiny silver wire to the hook snagged in the man's coattails.

"Hey!" shouted Quentin. "Come back. I got you out of the well. The least you could do is tell me who you are."

Without thinking he hauled back on the fishing pole. The little man was yanked backward onto the grass.

"Oh, I'm sorry," Quentin said. "I just wanted to get to know you."

And then he gasped in surprise. The thing at the end of his fishing pole was no longer the little man, but a scaly green dragon, fiercely rattling the plates of its body and lashing its tail. It blew fire and smoke from the pipe between its pointed teeth, and on its head was a dented top hat. The dragon pulled hard on the line, but frightened as

he was, Quentin kept a tight grip on the pole.

As he pulled, the dragon began to slide toward him through the grass. Then it changed from a dragon to a hideous green serpent, hissing loudly through the pipe in its mouth and finding it hard, with neither arms nor legs, to keep its battered hat from sliding over its eyes.

The dragon soon changed into a green unicorn. The unicorn in turn became an ugly vulture with green feathers and a pipe clamped in its beak.

Quentin became less and less frightened as the parade of beasts kept appearing at the end of his fishing line. He noticed that whatever form the hooked thing took, it never turned to attack him. It was always trying to get away.

He finally pulled close to him a seven-headed green dog with a hat on each of the heads and a pipe in each of the mouths. The dog yipped as Quentin reached out a hand. Then, just as he was about to touch it, the dog with seven heads disappeared. In its place was the little man, sitting near Quentin's feet.

"I . . . I just wanted to talk." Quentin sat down beside the man. "Besides, you shouldn't be running around all wet. You'll catch cold."

"I wonder if you'd be so kind as to take the hook out of my clothing," said the man. "It's hard to reach back there."

"No," replied Quentin stubbornly. "First tell me who you are."

The little man shook his head sadly. "So that's the way of it," he whispered. "No good will come of this. But if you must know . . . I'm called Flan."

"Flan. That's an odd name." Quentin put out his hand again. "How do you do, Mr. Flan?"

"Not 'mister,' " said the little man, taking Quentin's first two fingers in his tiny fist. "Just Flan."

"Oh, you mean that's your first name? Then what's . . . ?"

"Flan. That's the only name I come with. Now you caught me fair and square, and made me tell who I am. But haven't you ever heard of anybody with just one name before?"

"No. But I never saw anybody with green skin before, either."

"Oh, really?" Flan got to his feet and drew himself up to his full height of almost eighteen inches. "Now don't go making fun of me because of my color. Green's just as good as black or white or purple or gold or whatever other colors skin comes in these days. In fact, I think green's a rather becoming color. Don't you?"

"But green . . ." Quentin began.

"Oh, what's another color more or less between friends, eh?"

Quentin frowned. "You may be in for trouble.

21

Poppa says that sometimes people with different-colored skins don't get on too well together."

"The first person who tries something with me because of my color," Flan snapped, "I'll give him green skin, I will. I'll turn him into a frog."

Quentin swallowed loudly. "You . . . you could do that?"

"Sure. I can do all sorts of magic. Look."

He reached into the air. And there, between his fingers, appeared a bright silver coin.

"Getting rid of it isn't hard, either." Flan tossed the coin high into the air. Glittering in the sun, it reached the top of its flight . . . and disappeared.

"Can you bring it back again?"

"Of course. Just look in your hand."

Inside his closed fist, Quentin could feel the coin. He opened his fingers. The coin looked foreign. There seemed to be a picture of a king on it. But the king was puffing on a pipe. And the crown on his head looked very much like a top hat.

"Keep it, lad. There's plenty more where that came from."

"What . . . what kind of a person are you?" Quentin gasped, turning the coin over and over and finally putting it into his pocket.

Flan rubbed at his chin. "I'm what folks would call a leprechaun."

"A what?"

"Leprechaun. Lepp . . . ri . . . kawn. One of the wee folk. All of us come from Ireland, and we're given to playing pranks and doing magic. Now there's certain benefits from catching one of us and learning his name. But problems can arise, too."

"Benefits? What benefits? And if you're from Ireland, what are you doing here? And how did you get down the well? And . . ."

"Whoa, lad. Whoa. First of all, I'm not in Ireland anymore because I wanted to see the world. Ireland's beautiful, mind. But after a few hundred years there, I had a yearning to see new lands."

"A . . . few . . . hundred . . . years?" Quentin said slowly.

"Oh yes. We leprechauns live forever, you know. Anyway, one day I hid in a ship bound around the world. But by the time it reached this country, my poor stomach had enough of sailing, thank you. I roamed around and finally found what I thought was a nice home."

"A home? Where?"

"In the village yonder."

"Cedar Ferry?"

"Aye, that's it. I found a cozy nook under a porch. A family of mice was already living there, but when I told them of my needs, they were ever so nice about moving out."

"But how did you get down the well?"

23

"I'm coming to that. You see the porch I was living under belonged to a Mrs. Viola Trussker."

Then Quentin remembered what Vincent had told him about the face at Mrs. Trussker's window and the other happenings in the village last night. He hadn't believed a word of it. But here was the green man himself.

"Finally, living under that porch got to be too much to bear."

"How come?"

"It was her singing. She practiced every evening. And her whooping and shrieking about deafened me. And then last night she sang 'I Love You Truly' for fully an hour. I had to leave before the horrible noise made me lose my senses. Before going, I peeked in through the window to see if one human being could possibly make all that racket."

"And she saw you."

Flan nodded.

"And the thing running across the lawn. That was you, too, wasn't it?"

"I thought the old man was asleep. I was taking a shortcut."

"But the tiger's roar. Everybody heard it. What about that?"

Flan opened his mouth. Out came the croak of a frog, a horse's whinny, the trumpeting of an elephant, a parrot's screeching cry . . . and finally, the roar of a Bengal tiger.

"It works fine for scaring off curious dogs." Flan grinned. "But after all that excitement, I couldn't stay. So I set off. The old schoolhouse seemed a good place to settle in. But as I came near, the ground gave way beneath my feet. I tumbled into the well, and there's where you found me."

"Flan?"

"Yes, lad?"

"If you can do all kinds of magic, why didn't you get yourself out of the well? Why did you need me to help you?"

Flan snapped his fingers and a flicker of flame appeared at the end of his thumb. He stuck the thumb into the bowl of his pipe and puffed out thick clouds of smoke.

"I couldn't get out of the well," he said, "because I once fell asleep in school."

"School?"

"Of course, lad. By the time I was your age—centuries ago—I'd already studied how to cast spells and get rid of demons and cause folks to see the unseeable. All sorts of things."

Oh, how Quentin wished he could go to a school like that!

"But what does falling asleep in school have to do with getting out of a well?" he asked.

"I was sitting way in the back of the class, and the teacher was explaining how to fly. The magic spell was fearful complicated, and the day was hot, and I was tired. So I just drifted off to sleep. Worse yet, I started to snore. That angered the teacher so, he vowed he'd never allow me to make up the lesson. So I'm one of the few leprechauns in the world who can't—no matter what happens—fly."

Flan shook his head sadly. "It's the shame of my life. All the other leprechauns gliding gracefully through the air. But I never learned how. So you see, there was no way out of the well until you came by."

He sucked thoughtfully at his pipe for several moments. From time to time he breathed long sighs that seemed to come up from the very soles of his shoes. "And now, lad," he said finally, "you must claim your due."

"My due?" asked Quentin.

"You caught me fair and square, and you made me say my name. Now if we were back in Ireland, I'd have to give you a pot of gold."

"A pot of gold! Oh, that would be . . ."

"Hold on, lad. I didn't bring the gold with me on my voyage."

"No gold," said Quentin sadly. "Then . . ."

"But I must give up something to him who finds out my name. That's the Law of the Leprechauns."

26

"What?" Quentin asked eagerly. "What must you give me?"

"I must grant you three wishes."

Three wishes! Quentin let his breath out with a rush. Three wishes. He'd read about such things in books. But he never dreamed it could really happen. Especially to him.

"Can I wish for anything?" he asked.

"Anything at all," Flan replied. "But I'd best warn you. Whatever you wish for, that's what you get. And you'll have it for all time. Unless, of course, you use another wish to undo the first one. I heard of a man once who used his third wish to know the day he was to die. That's a terrible thing for anyone to know. He'd have given anything to take back that wish. But he'd made it, and he was stuck with it. So have a care, Quentin. Use your wishes wisely."

Quentin nodded. "I guess I'd better think about it for a little while," he said.

Off in the west, the late afternoon sun was settling toward the horizon. "I'd better be getting home," said Quentin, still filled with the wonder of having the three wishes. "Will you come with me, Flan?"

"Don't mind if I do," the little man replied. "Though I'm a bit uneasy inside houses. Some folks find my appearance a bit odd."

"You can stay in the barn," said Quentin. "There's a big haymow to rest in."

A huge smile lit Flan's face. "A haymow? All warm and soft? Lead the way, lad."

Quentin picked up his bike at the edge of the road and sighed. He'd completely forgotten about the flat tire.

"Now then." Flan rubbed his hands together. "How far is it to that cozy barn?"

"Nearly four miles. I wish my bike was fixed. Then we'd be there in no time."

There was a rumble of thunder, and the air itself seemed to shake as if a big invisible door had been slammed.

With a hissing sound the bike's flat tire filled with air.

Startled, Quentin looked at the bike and then at Flan.

"First wish granted," said the little man. "Hop aboard. That basket up front looks just big enough for me."

Flan curled up in the basket, and Quentin started pedaling. It isn't fair, he thought to himself. One wish used already.

"I wish there was a way to keep from making wishes I really don't want to," he muttered in a low voice.

"Easy as pie, Quentin," chuckled Flan, who was

enjoying the rush of wind in his face. "Tell you what. We won't consider the third wish fully made until you count to three after you've made it. Before you do that, you can cancel if you like."

"Hey, that's a great idea, Flan. That way I won't . . ."

Suddenly Quentin stared at the little man. The bike almost went into the ditch.

"What do you mean, my third wish?" Quentin cried angrily. "What happened to the second one?"

"You just had it, wishing not to make silly wishes," chuckled Flan. "One more left. Think wisely on it."

Now Quentin found it very hard to think at all. A moment ago he'd had three wishes, and now there was only one left. He'd have to be very careful with it. What would it be?

A new bike? No, that wasn't nearly enough. Flan said he could wish for *anything*. And there were so many things he wanted.

The new bike . . . the fishing rod? Something for Momma and Poppa? That was better. Perhaps he could wish for all of Poppa's debts to be paid. And with a little bit of money left over to buy something nice for . . .

Money! The more Quentin thought about it, the better the idea seemed. With enough money he could buy anything. He could buy lots of things. Of course. He'd wish for . . . for . . .

"Flan?"

"Yes, Quentin?"

"I . . . I think I'll take my third wish now."

"I see." Flan stared at Quentin for a long moment. "Have you given it all the thought a serious matter like this needs?"

Quentin nodded. He knew what he wanted more than anything else.

"Very well," said Flan. "Just make your wish. And don't forget to count to three afterward. That way we'll both know it's a true wish."

"All right." Quentin closed his eyes.

"I wish . . ." he said very softly, "I wish for all the money in the world. One . . . two . . . THREE!"

For a moment there was only silence. Then a tremendous *whumph*, followed by noises as if the sky itself were tearing apart. Even with his eyes closed, Quentin seemed to see the sun and the stars wobbling in their paths through the heavens.

Finally the awful quiet. A quiet which was broken by Flan's voice, solemn and filled with wonder.

"Open your eyes, Quentin. Your wish has been granted."

# 3
# All the Money in the World

Slowly Quentin opened his eyes and looked about. There were the fields, and a cow in a pasture was grazing contentedly. Down the road he could see the old schoolhouse.

But no money. Not a dollar. Not a dime. Not even a penny.

"It was all just talk, wasn't it, Flan?" said Quentin sadly. "There's no money."

"I wouldn't trick you, lad," Flan answered. "You wanted all the money in the world, and you've got it. But it comes to a bit more than you'd want to carry on your person. And you'd not want all that money lying at the edge of the road out here."

Disappointed, Quentin pedaled slowly along the road toward the farm. Maybe all the money in the world was too much to wish for. Perhaps he should have settled for a new bike. A ten-speed, like Roselynn and Vincent had.

He pushed hard against the pedals and guided his bike up the last rise in the road. His house was just over the hill. Poppa would probably be out in the barn, and Momma would be in the house, starting to fix supper.

31

The house came into view. Quentin barely looked at it. But then he looked again. There was something beyond it. Something in the fields where Poppa had planted his crops.

His eyes grew wide then, and he began to shake all over. Just this morning, out beyond the barn, there had been acre after acre of tomato plants and beans and cabbages, looking green and fresh against the brown earth.

But now there wasn't a plant to be seen. All over the farm, wide fields were covered up by huge mounds of—of *something*. The mounds were higher even than the rooster weather vane on the big barn, and they blocked out the afternoon sun. As the breeze blew against them, whatever was in those mounds rustled and clinked.

It was . . . it was . . .

"All the money in the world!" Quentin shouted joyfully.

He ran excitedly to the nearest pile. He looked up—way up to the top of the mountain of paper which seemed almost as high as the clouds. He plunged his arms into the base of the pile, and a small landslide of dollar bills slid down on him.

Laughing and shouting for Flan to join him, Quentin pushed his way through more loose bills to the next pile. And on to the next. And the next.

There were English pounds and Indian rupees and French francs and Mexican pesos and Portuguese escudos and Spanish pesetas and Dutch guilders and German marks—so many kinds of money.

He made his way around several silvery mounds of coins which were standing next to neat stacks of gold bars. It was impossible for him to see where he was. As he stood, knee deep in coins and bills, the mountains of money on all sides loomed over him. He could no longer see the house or the barn. He was lost. Lost amid all the money in the world.

Ahead he saw countless piles of green U.S. money. Some of it was neatly wrapped with rubber bands or paper strips. Other loose bills crunched beneath his feet as he walked.

Flan had disappeared somewhere. Quentin wandered about, looking for him. Finally he came to the fence at the edge of the road, where he found the little man seated on the top rail with a wide grin on his face.

"See, lad?" he said. "I kept my promise, didn't I?"

Quentin nodded. He looked across the road. No money there. The piles of money stopped at the edge of the road where Poppa's farm ended.

"Well, Quentin," Flan went on, "the bargain's complete, and there's nothing left to keep me here. I'll be off to the barn and that comfortable haymow you . . ."

"Quentin? What are you doing out here, boy?"

At the sound of the deep voice behind them, both Quentin and Flan jumped.

"Poppa?" Quentin turned about slowly, a scared look on his face.

"That's right, Quentin. And I want to know what's going on. Where did all those big piles of stuff come from? They weren't here an hour ago when I was out hoeing. Our crops will be crushed flat with all that stuff piled on them. Do you know anything about this?"

Quentin's father was six feet tall, with a chest like a barrel and arms and legs as hard as oak logs. Flan took one look at his angry face and scuttled into an opening between two piles of money.

"What was that?" said Mr. Stowe, catching a glimpse of the little man. He shoved his arm in among the bills.

"Yi!" Flan was dragged out by one leg and dangled head down as Mr. Stowe lifted him up for an inspection. The little man immediately changed into a green dragon, but the dragon was fetched such a clout by Mr. Stowe's free hand that he quickly changed back again.

"Aren't you kind of small to be smoking?" asked Mr. Stowe, looking at the pipe in Flan's mouth.

"Put me down this instant," Flan yipped, "or I'll . . . I'll change you into a frog."

This brought another slap from Mr. Stowe. "I'll put you down," he said. "But only if you promise not to run away."

"All right, I promise. After all, I only granted what Quentin wished for."

"Oh?" Mr. Stowe placed Flan on the ground. "Is he a friend of yours, Quentin? Is he responsible for burying my crops under all this stuff?"

"Poppa, we've got something better than crops," said Quentin. "We've got *all the money in the world*!"

"That's foolish talk, boy," said Mr. Stowe with a shake of his head. "All this paper and things can't be worth a hill of beans." He bent down and picked up a gold coin from the ground.

"But it's real, Poppa! It is!"

"A green man," Mr. Stowe said thoughtfully. "And all the money in the world? Farm's a mess, and it'll take weeks to clear it off. It's like the bad dreams I have when I eat too much of your momma's mustard pickle, Quentin. I think we'd better go up to the house and let her hear about this. She'll be able to make some sense of it, I'm sure."

With Flan on his shoulder, Quentin walked beside Poppa back toward the house. The screen door to the kitchen banged as they went inside.

Momma was at the oven. As she turned about,

dusting flour from her hands, she immediately caught sight of Flan.

"Why, isn't he the cutest thing!" Mrs. Stowe reached out and plucked the little man from Quentin's shoulder. Then she planted a big kiss on his green cheek.

"Stop it, woman!" Flan cried. "Enough of that!"

To tell the truth, he rather enjoyed the kiss, but no true leprechaun would ever admit such a thing.

"We've got some darn stuff piled up all over the farm," Mr. Stowe told his wife. "Mounds higher than the house. Higher than the trees, even."

"What, George?" asked Mrs. Stowe. "What is it?"

"I already told Poppa," Quentin interrupted. "It's money—all the money in the world."

"And I suppose Cinderella is coming for supper tonight," snapped Mrs. Stowe. "Quentin, when you start with this daydreaming business, I just want to walk out of the room so I won't have to listen."

"But I'm telling the truth, Momma. I am!"

Mr. Stowe dug into his pocket and pulled out the coin. "Here, Ruth. I found it on one of those piles. Looks like gold, doesn't it?"

She weighed the coin in her hand. Then she nicked it with her paring knife. And when she turned back to her husband, her eyes were wide.

"It's soft metal, and heavy," she said. "First I thought it was lead with gold paint over it. But it's yellow all the way through."

"Do you think it's gold, then?" asked Mr. Stowe.

Slowly his wife nodded her head. She went to the kitchen door and opened it.

"There's something out there, right enough. But all the money in the world? It can't be."

From the pasture just beyond the barnyard came the sound of cows bellowing and horses whinnying.

"Look." Mr. Stowe pointed. "That pile of gold bars has blocked off the creek by the fence. It can't flow through to the pasture. Our poor animals are getting thirsty. Come on, Quentin. We've got to do something about that."

"George," said Mrs. Stowe. "It'll take you a week to get the creek flowing again."

"But we've got to do something now. Quentin, you fetch some buckets from the barn. We're going to have to tote water for those animals."

"But why do we have to work when . . . ?" Quentin took one look at the scowl on his father's face and plodded off toward the barn to get the buckets.

It didn't seem fair, somehow. Hauling water to the animals was hard work. Too hard to be done by a boy who had all the money in the world.

Down by the fence where the creek was dammed, the water made a little pond. Mr. Stowe filled two of the buckets and handed them to Quentin. Then he filled two more to carry himself.

By the time they'd carried enough water for all the animals, Quentin's back and arms were one big ache, and he could hardly stand up.

"We'll have to do it again in the morning," his father told him. As they walked back toward the barn, the money rustled and clinked underfoot. "Money or no money, the animals need their water."

Quentin tried to catch his breath and talk at the same time. "Couldn't we . . . just . . . hire somebody to tote water? Or have pipes put in? There's enough money here to do anything we want."

"If it really is money," answered his father doubtfully. "But putting in pipe takes time, and hired help isn't easy to come by this time of year."

"Hi, Quentin."

As Quentin walked around the corner of the barn he almost bumped into Vincent and Roselynn. Beyond them he could see a long line of cars parked next to the road. People were standing beside them, staring about and muttering to one another. There was Mr. Cristobell and his wife. And Mr. and Mrs. Barclay. And the whole Pepperidge family.

It seemed as if half the village had turned out to gape at the heaps and mounds of money covering the Stowe farm.

"What . . . what is it?" Roselynn gasped.

"It's all the money in the world," Quentin replied proudly.

For a moment, Roselynn and Vincent were silent, trying to understand what Quentin had just told them. Then Vincent let out a yell.

"Wow! Oh, wow! Think of all the things you'll be able to buy!"

"Think of what *we'll* be able to buy," Quentin replied. "Here, take some. I couldn't spend it all myself in a million years."

With that he reached into a mound of ten-dollar bills and began piling wads of them into Vincent's outstretched hands.

"Can . . . can I have some, too?" asked Roselynn.

"Sure," said Quentin. He tossed some bills into the air and laughed when Roselynn tried to catch them as they fluttered down.

"Now just hold on there." Quentin turned slowly when he heard Poppa's voice. "I don't think you'd better be giving away any of this money, Quentin. Not just yet, anyway."

"Why not, Poppa? Roselynn and Vincent are my friends."

"I know. But I'd feel a lot easier about all this if

we just let the money sit here awhile. At least until we can find out where it came from."

With sad little sighs, Roselynn and Vincent opened their fists and allowed the money to fall to the ground.

Mr. Cristobell walked over to Quentin. "Not likely the money's real," he said. He was holding a stack of bills with a strip of paper around them. "Look here. These have foreign printing on them. You can't even read it."

He jammed the bills into his pocket.

"Hey, put them back!" Quentin cried. "It's not fair. If my friends can't have any money, you have no right to . . ."

Roughly, Mr. Cristobell shoved Quentin aside and plunged his hands into a pile of gold coins.

And then Mr. Cristobell seemed to leap backward. Quentin looked up to see Poppa holding him firmly by a shoulder.

"Money or no money, Ed Cristobell—nobody shoves my son around. Especially when he's standing right here on our own land."

"Sorry, George," gasped Mr. Cristobell. "I guess I forgot myself. Please let me go."

In the scuffle Mr. Cristobell managed to jam a handful of gold coins into his pocket. All along the fence Mr. Stowe saw people from the town shoving coins and bills into pockets and purses.

"Now you just stop that!" he called. "I know most of you folks. But you're getting me kind of angry. So you just put that money back. Otherwise I'm going to forget we're friends and deal with you like I would a bunch of common thieves."

The people looked at him, ashamed. And the money was returned. All except a single coin which Mr. Cristobell hid in his pocket.

"Now git!" snapped Mr. Stowe. "Off my property. Everybody!"

The people took one look at his angry face and huge arms. Then they raced off toward their cars.

"Can Vincent and I come back tomorrow to see the money?" Roselynn whispered in Quentin's ear.

He nodded and stared at the pile of gold coins at the edge of the road.

And then, just as Mr. Cristobell stepped onto the road to return to his car, Quentin heard a tiny *click*. That was strange. It seemed to him that one more coin had appeared magically at the very top of the pile. But that couldn't be, he thought. He must have imagined it.

A mile down the road, Mr. Cristobell stopped his car. He smiled at his wife and pushed his hand deep into his pocket.

But then the smile vanished. His fingers felt about, and finally he turned the pocket inside out. It had no hole in it. And there was no way the coin could have fallen out. He'd been too careful for that.

The gold coin he'd taken from the Stowe farm had simply disappeared.

# 4
# *Callers*

Quentin was awake most of that night. He kept looking out the window at the piles of money in the moonlight. And when he finally did get to sleep, it seemed that almost at once his father was shaking him awake.

"Six-thirty, Quentin," Mr. Stowe said. "We've got to haul more water for the animals."

Quentin groaned. He still ached from carrying the heavy buckets yesterday. He wondered if all rich people had to work this hard. If so, what was the use of having all the money in the world?

By the time they finished, Quentin was so stiff he could hardly stand up. He limped into the kitchen. Flan was seated in the old high chair that Quentin had used as a baby. Momma had given him a piece of cherry pie.

Flan forked the last bit of it into his mouth and then picked up the plate. He began licking at the sweet juice with his tongue. Mrs. Stowe just laughed at him. Quentin didn't think that was quite fair. If he'd done the same thing, Momma would have whacked him one for sure.

"Guess what, George," said Mrs. Stowe. "Flan has decided to stay on with us for a while. Isn't that nice?"

"Uh-huh," said Mr. Stowe doubtfully. "I suspect it's more cherry pie than friendship that's keeping him here. I don't know that we're in any position to take on a boarder right now, Ruth."

"Well I like him. So he stays. I've made up my mind, George Stowe."

When Momma called Poppa "George Stowe" like that, it was usually the end of any argument.

"All right," said Mr. Stowe. "But Quentin, don't you take to smoking a pipe just because Flan does. He's a lot older than you are."

"Three hundred and twenty-six," Flan said. "Come September."

Quentin laughed at the look on Poppa's face.

From outside they heard the sound of a car pulling into the driveway. A few seconds later the front doorbell rang. Momma went to answer.

"George . . . Quentin?" she called. "There are some men from the village to see you."

They got up and went into the living room. Quentin recognized the three men standing just inside the front door.

The tall thin one in the wool shirt was Roscoe Peabody, Roselynn's father. He owned the Cedar Ferry Hardware Store and was honorary mayor of the little village.

The heavy man in the blue uniform was Vincent's father, Gavin Arbor. His silver sheriff's star glittered on his shirt pocket.

The short fat man in the gray suit was James Sedgewick, the president of the Cedar Ferry National Bank.

Sheriff Arbor was the first to speak. "George, something strange is going on. And it's making me a lot of trouble. Seems you've suddenly got a lot of money piled up here on your farm."

"Yeah. And it's ruining my crops. I wish I could think of a way to get rid of it," Mr. Stowe answered.

"Well, people driving by are stopping to look at it. Earlier this morning the traffic was backed up all the way into town. I had to call in the state police just to get things moving again."

*"Traffic!"* roared Mr. Sedgewick. "Is that all you're worried about, Gavin? Every bit of money in my bank was gone this morning, and all you can talk about is *traffic?*"

"Now cool down, both of you," snapped Roscoe Peabody. "As the mayor of Cedar Ferry, I want to keep this little talk nice and orderly. Now then,

George, we know you're not a thief. But suppose you tell us where all that money came from."

"I got it," came a voice from the kitchen doorway. "For Quentin."

*"What in the living blue blazes is that?"* Banker Sedgewick's eyes were round with astonishment, and his face was as white as a ghost. The others turned toward where his finger was wildly pointing.

Flan stood in the doorway. His eyes twinkled merrily. From the pipe in his mouth came huge clouds of smoke.

"He . . . he's green!" Mr. Sedgewick gasped.

"And he's no taller than my knee," added Mr. Peabody.

"But he's smoking a pipe." Sheriff Arbor slapped a hand to his forehead. He wondered if he were having a bad dream.

" 'Twas me that brought the money to the farm," said Flan. "So if there's any problems, you can discuss them with me."

"Arbor," said Mr. Sedgewick, "he must have stolen it—and some of it from my bank. That's against the law. So do your duty."

"And what would you have the sheriff do, Mr. Sedgewick?" Flan asked. "Put me in jail?"

"Why . . ." Mr. Sedgewick thought about this. "Why, yes."

"The jail hasn't been made that can hold a leprechaun."

"A what?"

"A leprechaun. I'm a distant relative of the gnomes, trolls, and goblins. And even if you put me in prison, you'd have a terrible time keeping me there."

With that, he began walking toward the front wall of the living room.

"Watch out! You'll bump into . . ." Sheriff Arbor was suddenly silent. Like the others, he watched in amazement as the little man walked through the wall as if it weren't there at all.

Flan called to them from the front porch. "Still think you can keep me in jail?"

Mr. Peabody took out a handkerchief and wiped his forehead as Flan came back through the wall and climbed onto Quentin's shoulder.

"There . . . there sure is a lot of money out there," said Mr. Sedgewick. "Is it all real?"

Quentin nodded. "It's all the money in the world."

"Quentin, you hush up that kind of talk," said his father. "You men know how Quentin is when he gets to daydreaming."

"A lot of money," Sedgewick repeated. "Can you imagine the sort of place Cedar Ferry could be with that kind of money in its bank?"

"We could build a new police station," said Sheriff Arbor. "And get more police cars, and . . . and . . ."

"Why, we could put up the biggest city hall in the state. In the whole country!" added Mayor Peabody.

"All kinds of businesses would move in if they knew they could get loans from our bank," said Sedgewick. "Cedar Ferry would grow. We wouldn't be just a little village anymore. We'd be a city! Bigger than New York or Chicago. If we spent that money in the right way, we could . . ."

"Aren't you forgetting something?" asked Mr. Stowe.

"What?" Mr. Sedgewick was still dreaming of what his bank could do with all that money.

"The money had to come from somewhere," said Mr. Stowe. "Isn't that right, Flan?"

"Course it did," chirped the little man. "But now it's all Quentin's."

"But all that money—somebody should be told where it is. Somebody important."

"Why, Poppa?" Quentin asked. "If the money's mine, why do we have to tell anybody about it?"

Mr. Stowe closed his eyes and thought for a moment. "I'm not much good at money matters," he said finally. "But all that money . . . people should know about it. People who'd know what to do next."

"Who would you tell?" asked Sheriff Arbor. "The governor?"

"I was thinking of going a little higher than that." Mr. Stowe looked squarely at Quentin. "How about it? If you really believe all that belongs to you, you shouldn't be scared to let people know about it."

Quentin *was* scared. Scared that somehow he'd lose all his money. But he didn't dare tell Poppa that.

"All right," he said. His eyes began prickling with tears.

"Good boy." Mr. Stowe patted Quentin on the back and then picked up the telephone. He twisted the dial once. "Hello, Lois?" he said to the operator. "I want you to get me the White House. Yes, the White House in Washington, D.C. That's right. I want to talk to the President of the United States."

He waited at the phone for several minutes while Arbor, Peabody, and Sedgewick whispered among themselves. They were important men in Cedar Ferry, but none of them had ever dreamed of calling the President.

Finally Mr. Stowe handed the telephone to Quentin. "They're ringing now," he said.

Quentin put the receiver to his ear. "Hello? Hello, is this the White House?"

"Is it the President?" whispered Peabody.

Quentin shook his head nervously. "It's some-body named Mr. Gibson or Mr. Gilson. He says he's an assistant or an aide or . . . or . . . something like that."

"Now calm down," said Poppa. "Mind your manners. First tell him who you are and where you live."

Quentin did as he was told. "Mr. Gilson is writing all this down," he whispered to Poppa. Then he talked into the phone again.

"Yes, sir, it is important. . . . You see, I have all the money in the world here on the farm, and . . . No, I'm not trying to be funny. . . . I know the President is a busy man, but . . . Yes, it's about three miles south of the village. . . . You can't miss it. . . . It's the place with all the money piled up. . . . If you'd just tell the President . . . Yes, sir, I see. . . ."

Everyone in the room heard the squawking voice coming from the telephone receiver. "Yes, sir," said Quentin weakly. "Yes, sir."

He hung up the telephone.

"What did that Gilson fellow say?" Peabody asked eagerly.

"First he wanted to know how I'd heard that there was money missing," said Quentin. "It was supposed to be a secret, he said."

"A secret?" Sedgewick shook his head. "Nobody

51

could keep that much money vanishing a secret. What else did he tell you, Quentin?"

"He said the President was getting lots of reports of money disappearing. And I was the fifty-eighth call about where it is. One man told about seeing it carried off in a flying saucer."

"Some people will do just anything for a little attention," said Mr. Stowe angrily. "But aren't they going to look into your story, Quentin?"

Quentin nodded. "Mr. Gilson didn't sound like he believed me. But he said the army would investigate."

"You should have spoken to the President himself," said Peabody. "Maybe you could have convinced him."

"The President wasn't there. Mr. Gilson said he's getting ready to go on television."

"TV!" said Mr. Arbor. "Where's the set, George?"

They rushed into the living room. Mr. Stowe turned on the TV just in time.

"Ladies and gentlemen," came a voice from the speaker, "the President of the United States."

Bright lights flashed on the TV screen. And then Quentin saw a man in a blue suit. His hair was gray, and he was seated behind a big desk. On the front of the desk was a round sign with a picture of an eagle on it.

"That's the President, Quentin," said Mr. Stowe.

"Today," said the President, "something has happened which has never before occurred in history. The whole money supply of Washington, D.C., has disappeared. I repeat, your government is without the money needed to carry on its business. We have reports of money missing from other parts of the country, so we don't know the total amount that's gone. And we can't tell how it happened.

"Until we can find the money, most government work will have to stop. The situation is serious but not hopeless. I'm sure we'll be able to borrow, either from this country's banks or from foreign countries."

"Foreign banks?" Mr. Stowe looked suddenly at Quentin. "How much money did you say was out there on our farm?"

"All the money in the world," Quentin answered.

"He really believes it," chuckled Sedgewick. "The boy really thinks he's got all the money in the world."

From the TV, the President's voice continued.

"To locate the missing money," he went on, "I have appointed Major General Linus Mainwaring. General Mainwaring will do whatever is necessary to find and return the money to where it belongs."

53

The President turned to someone on his left. "General Mainwaring, do you have anything to say?"

The camera turned slightly, and General Mainwaring looked toward it. His mouth was an angry slit, and his face reminded Quentin of a bulldog's.

"You bet I do, Mr. President. I just want to say this to whoever has that money. You had to be pretty smart to get it. But we're going to find you, mister. And when we do—watch out!"

General Mainwaring's picture faded from the TV screen. Quentin was beginning to get a little frightened. Having all the money in the world wasn't as much fun as he'd thought it would be.

In fact, up to now it hadn't been any fun at all.

# 5
# The Army Arrives

That afternoon Vincent and Roselynn came by to play with Quentin. Naturally they wanted to play among the piles of money. Quentin was glad for something to get his mind off General Mainwaring and what he'd said on the TV.

Vincent ran to the base of a huge mound of twenty-dollar bills. He scooped up an armful of money and tossed it into the air. "Ice-cream sodas!" he cried as the bills rained back down on him. "Thousands of ice-cream sodas!"

"I'd rather have a trail bike with a real engine than all the sodas in the world," said Roselynn. She folded one bill into a paper airplane and glided it over a pile of silver coins. "And maybe a pair of racing skis with boots and poles, and a new stereo set."

Quentin, with Flan beside him, watched them. He had never been so happy. Lots of times Roselynn and Vincent had let him borrow a bike or a fishing pole or a baseball glove. Here was his chance to do something for them.

"Hey, come here," he said. "Both of you. I've got an idea."

"What kind of an idea, Quent?" Roselynn asked.

"It's a game. You've got to see how much money you can carry. And no hands allowed. C'mon, Roselynn. You first."

He picked up a handful of money and crammed it into a pocket of Roselynn's jacket. "That's it. Pack it down really tight."

"No fair," said Vincent. "I didn't wear a jacket."

"Put some of these inside your shirt then." Quentin began tossing stacks of bills at Vincent. "That's it. It's money time!"

By the time Roselynn and Vincent had finished stuffing money into their clothes, they both looked round, fat, and lumpy. Vincent, with the twenty-dollar bills sticking out from between the buttons of his shirt, reminded Quentin of a scarecrow Poppa had once made of clothes filled with straw. He roared with laughter.

"Fat ol' Vince and fat ol' Roselynn! You two should see yourselves."

"But what do we do now, Quent?" Vincent asked. "With the money, I mean."

"You take it home with you. It's yours."

Roselynn looked wide-eyed at Vincent and then slowly turned back to Quentin. "But . . . but are you sure it's all right?"

"It's my money, isn't it? I can do anything I want with it. And right now I want to give some of it to my best friends."

"Oh, wow!" Vincent howled wildly. "Wow! All this money for me. Yippee!"

He threw his arms wide. Then he ran to the base of the mound of twenty-dollar-bills and began scrambling up the side of it.

"Look at me!" he called from the top. "King of the money hill!"

"Oh, Quentin," said Roselynn. "You're just so . . . so . . ."

And before he could stop her she leaned forward and kissed him on the cheek.

"Hey, cut that out!" Quentin rubbed his cheek

with his fingers. Before he could decide whether or not he liked being kissed by Roselynn, there was a shout from Vincent.

"Trucks!" From the top of the heap of money, Vincent was pointing off down the road. "Lots of trucks. Coming this way."

Quentin struggled up the side of the pile until he was standing beside Vincent. "What's going on?" called Flan from down below.

A whole line of trucks was coming down the road. They were brown, or perhaps green. The backs had cloth over them, like covered wagons.

"Look," said Vincent. "On the sides of the trucks. It says U.S. ARMY."

The army? Quentin and Vincent slid down the pile of money to the ground. Quentin didn't like the idea of army trucks coming to the farm.

As the first truck passed the piles of money, the driver pointed over to the side. The truck pulled off the road. The second truck came up behind it and stopped. The trucks kept pulling over and stopping, and pretty soon there was a long line of them, mashing the grass by the fence.

Quentin crouched with Flan, Vincent, and Roselynn behind a heap of British pound notes. From his hiding place he watched a man in uniform get out of the first truck. He knew the man was a sergeant because of the three stripes on his sleeve.

Poppa had been a sergeant in the army once, and he'd been proud of the stripes he'd worn.

"Dis . . . mount!" shouted the sergeant. From the back of each of the trucks men wearing uniforms and helmets began jumping to the ground. They were carrying rifles too, and that was scary.

"Atten . . . hut!" yelled the sergeant. The men lined up facing the road. They stood very straight, their rifles hanging from straps over their shoulders.

Along the road came a shiny black car with a flag attached to the front fender. It screeched to a stop near the head of the line of trucks. The driver got out and opened the rear door.

A man got out of the backseat. Quentin gasped. The man was in uniform, but instead of a helmet he wore a stiff army hat. On his chest was row after row of medals, and there were two brass stars on each of his shoulders. But what worried Quentin was the pistol in the holster strapped to his waist.

Quentin knew who the man was. Just that morning he had seen that face on the TV screen.

Major General Linus Mainwaring!

A second man got out of the car. On the shoulders of this man's uniform were gold bars.

"It's the money, all right," he said to the general. "Just where our observation plane said they'd spotted it."

General Mainwaring nodded, scowling at the heaps of bills all over the fields.

"Lieutenant," he rumbled, "tell the men to advance across the fence."

"Yes, sir." The lieutenant turned to the sergeant. "Tell the men to advance across the fence."

The sergeant saluted. "Yes, sir." He turned to the long line of soldiers. "Men!" he shouted in a high voice. "Advance across the fence!"

Quentin wondered why General Mainwaring didn't just tell the men himself instead of telling the lieutenant, who told the sergeant, who told the soldiers. Maybe, he thought, it was a rule to give the lieutenant and the sergeant something to do.

And then a very frightening thing happened. The soldiers started coming toward where Quentin and his friends were hiding. They walked between the trucks. Then they hopped over the fence and stood in a long line, facing the piles of money.

General Mainwaring was the last to come over the fence. He was so heavy that he had to be helped by the lieutenant and the sergeant. Huffing and puffing, he faced the soldiers.

"Surround the money," said General Mainwaring.

"Surround the money," said the lieutenant.

"Surround the money," said the sergeant.

The soldiers began to spread out. The sergeant took a radio from his truck and spoke into it. "Soldiers in place, north side—right! Soldiers in place, west side—right!"

It took nearly twenty minutes for the men to surround the entire farm. Roselynn and Vincent tried to keep very still so the money wouldn't rustle. Quentin felt Flan climbing up onto his shoulder. The little man's arm went about his neck.

"Hang on tight, Flan," he whispered.

General Mainwaring peered closely at the pile of money where Quentin and his friends were hiding. "I heard talking," he said in a voice that rumbled like thunder. "Is somebody in there?"

"Y . . . yes, sir," said Quentin in a tiny voice.

*"Then you come out here this instant!"*

Meekly Quentin shuffled out from behind the mound of money. Roselynn and Vincent followed him. They stood in a row before the general.

"You. You with that green thing on your shoulder. What's your name, young man?"

"Quentin . . . Quentin Stowe. And these are my friends, Vincent and Roselynn."

"Quentin Stowe, eh? And do you know how all this money got here?"

"Yes, mister . . . I mean, General. Flan brought it."

The general's face got red, and his cheeks jiggled with anger. "And what's a . . . a flan?"

"It's a who, sir." Quentin pointed to the little man on his shoulder.

"What is it? A monkey? A doll?"

"It's Flan, sir."

But General Mainwaring wasn't listening. His hand moved toward the holster at his belt. "Uh-oh," said Vincent. Roselynn gave a frightened little gasp.

Quentin was too scared to speak. But Flan merely smiled at the general and waved a hand toward the holster.

"Owww!" screamed the general. He yanked his hand upward. Out of the holster came a large lobster, its claw clamped tightly to the general's thumb.

With his free hand the general grasped the lobster's tail and tried to pull it away. Finally it released the thumb. The general threw it to the ground. It crawled a few steps and turned back into a pistol.

The nearby soldiers began laughing. Even Roselynn started to giggle.

"Stop that laughing!" General Mainwaring cried.

"Stop that laughing!" the lieutenant responded.

"Stop that laughing!" the sergeant ordered.

The laughing stopped.

"No more tricks, young man," the general growled. "You don't seem to realize that I'm here on orders from the President of the United States."

Even Flan seemed impressed by this.

"You two." General Mainwaring pointed at Roselynn and Vincent. "What on earth is making your clothes all lumpy like that?"

Vincent started to reach into his shirt to bring out some money.

"Keep your hands out where I can see them!" the general roared. He turned to the lieutenant. "He could have a hidden weapon."

"I doubt it, sir." The lieutenant hid a smile behind his hand. "He's just a boy."

"Perhaps. But he'll bear watching, all the same." General Mainwaring looked at Quentin again. "And just what were you three—you four—doing out here with all this money?"

"Just playing."

"Playing, eh? We'll see about that later. Sergeant, keep an eye on these people."

"Yes, sir."

"We will now proceed to load up the money," General Mainwaring announced. "We'll take the gold bars first."

"Wait!" cried Quentin. "The money's mine. You can't take it away."

"We can't, eh?" General Mainwaring turned to the lieutenant. "Load the first truck."

"Load the first truck."

"Load the first truck."

Several of the soldiers picked up gold bars, straining to carry them back over the fence to the first truck. Soon the truck was loaded. The back of it sagged under the weight of the heavy gold.

"Move the truck out."

"Move the truck out."

"Move the truck out."

The driver started the engine, and the truck pulled off the grass and out onto the road.

*Pong!*

The rear of the truck bounced up into the air. When it came back down, it was no longer sagging, and the tires were no longer pressed flat.

The driver stopped the truck. He got out and looked underneath. Finally he peered into the back, where the gold had been put.

"Sir, it . . . it's not there anymore," he called to General Mainwaring.

"What's not there?"

"The gold. It's gone."

The lieutenant tapped General Mainwaring on the shoulder. "It's not gone, sir," he said. "I don't know how it happened, but it's right there."

General Mainwaring looked just inside the

fence, where the lieutenant was pointing. He saw a pile of gold. But just a few seconds before, there had been no gold on that spot.

"You mean the gold came back?" snorted General Mainwaring. "Impossible!"

"Yes, sir," said the lieutenant. "But there it is."

For a moment the general scratched his chin and stared at the pile of gold. Then he turned to the lieutenant. "Pick up one of those gold bars," he ordered.

"Pick up one of those gold bars."

"Pick up one of . . ."

"Now stop that!" The general's face got very red. "You do it, Lieutenant."

"Yes, sir." The lieutenant picked up a gold bar.

"Carry it over to the fence and out onto the road."

Over the fence went the lieutenant. He walked until the toes of his shoes were right at the edge of the road.

"One more step, Lieutenant."

The lieutenant took the step. His shoe touched the tar surface of the road.

*Pong!*

Suddenly the lieutenant was no longer carrying the gold bar. It had disappeared from his hands.

And it was back on the pile by the fence.

General Mainwaring just stared at the pile of

gold bars. He couldn't believe his eyes.

"Lieutenant," he said, "I want you to have the men set up tents and make camp. We may be here awhile. Go over there in the woods on the other side of the road."

"Yes, sir. But what about the . . . the prisoners?"

"Oh. Oh, yes." General Mainwaring glowered down at the frightened little group.

"I can see a farmhouse over beyond the money," he said. "Which one of you lives there?"

"I do," Quentin answered. "And Flan is staying there, too."

"Very well, you remain. Sergeant, release the other two."

"Yes, sir." The sergeant looked down at Roselynn and Vincent. "Go on, you two," he said with a grin. "Get out of here."

"Yes, sir!" They both leaped to their feet and ran toward the fence. Inside their clothes, the money jiggled up and down at each step.

At the edge of the road, Vincent turned and waved. "So long, Quentin. Good luck."

Roselynn was the first to walk onto the road.

*Pong!*

Vincent was only a second behind her.

*Pong!*

And Quentin saw two things at almost the same time.

First, Vincent and Roselynn didn't look fat and lumpy anymore.

And second, there was a pile of twenty-dollar bills next to the returned gold.

"My money!" Roselynn cried. "It's gone. All gone."

"So's mine!" wailed Vincent. "And I was going to buy so many things. What happened?"

For a long time they just looked at one another, confused. Then Roselynn turned and pointed right at Quentin.

"I bet I know," she sneered. "It was him. He had Flan take all our money back."

Quentin jumped up. "Now wait a minute. I didn't . . ."

"Not much, you didn't," Roselynn interrupted.

"Yeah," Vincent added. "You never really meant us to have any money, did you?"

"I did. I really did."

"Come on, Vincent," said Roselynn. "Let's go get our bikes. We don't need his dumb old money. We can still have fun. Just the *two* of us."

And without looking back, they both ran up the road toward their bikes.

"My best friends!" Quentin looked after them. Then he kicked at some loose bills on the ground.

"Get the men started pitching their tents, Lieutenant," rumbled General Mainwaring. "I'm going up to the house and talk to the owner of this farm. Maybe I can get to the bottom of this money problem."

He stretched out an arm and beckoned to Quentin. "You, young man. You and that little green whatever-it-is. Come along with me."

# 6
# Homesick Money

There was no work for Mr. Stowe to do because all his fields were covered with money. So he was sitting in the kitchen, listening to the news on the radio. He didn't like what he heard.

"Banks and businesses all over the United States have reported that their money has disappeared. Even the small change in people's pockets and coins from children's piggy banks are gone.

"Our government has sent messages to both England and France asking to borrow money to aid the United States in this emergency. So far, there has been no reply from either country.

"Earlier today there was a rumor from the Pentagon that at least some of the missing money has been located. The President refused to comment on . . ."

There was a knock at the kitchen door, and Mr.

Stowe turned off the radio. Through the screen door he saw a man wearing the uniform of an army major general.

"Mr. Stowe?" said General Mainwaring.

"Yes, sir." Mr. Stowe got to his feet. "I'm glad the army's finally arrived. I'm ready to give you all the help I can with this money business."

The general didn't seem to hear him. He opened the door and came in, dragging Quentin behind him. Flan almost fell from Quentin's shoulder. The general's face was like an angry bulldog's.

"Is this your son?" he growled.

"Yes, that's him." Poppa's voice was low, but very serious. "And if you don't take your hands off him, you'll have me to deal with."

"I must tell you, Mr. Stowe, that I'm here on orders from the President of the United States!" barked the general.

"And I must remind you, sir," Poppa replied, "that you are standing in my house. Now that's all right as far as it goes. But don't come in here and try frightening my boy. Otherwise, out you go."

Quentin was amazed. Poppa had often talked to him about what it meant to be brave. And now he could see what Poppa meant. One man, standing up to a general with all those soldiers behind him. That was real bravery!

"But the President . . ." the general sputtered.

"I would tell the President the same thing," said Mr. Stowe. "Now why don't we sit down and talk about the money? There's coffee on the stove. And some pie that was just made yesterday."

"Pie?" What almost seemed to be a grin appeared on the general's face. "Homemade? Real pie?"

"That's right. Sit down and have a piece. Then we'll see what's to be done. I want that money off my beans and tomatoes just as much as you do."

The general sat at the kitchen table. Quentin poured coffee for Poppa and the general, and milk for Flan and himself. Mr. Stowe cut big wedges of pie for everybody.

"Good. Quite good," said General Mainwaring when he'd finished. "Now about the money, Mr. Stowe. I've never seen the President so upset. He has assigned every person under my command to guard your farm."

"Yes, I can see your trucks through the window," said Mr. Stowe. "There must be forty of them out there."

"And that's just a small part of this operation," the general went on. "There's a ring of soldiers around most of the county, roadblocks on all the highways, every river and stream watched. Even the cowpaths are guarded. And we have air force planes flying overhead and keeping watch. Nobody comes in or leaves unless I say so."

Roadblocks? Planes? Quentin couldn't believe his ears. "Why?" he asked.

"Because this farm is where the missing money seems to be. Before long, people are going to find that out. Then everybody will be rushing here. Reporters to get your story . . . bankers and factory owners who've lost the money that keeps them in business . . . thieves and robbers . . . and some folks who are just curious about what's going on. Without the army's protection, this place will be mobbed. It would be a dangerous situation. We can't let that happen."

Mr. Stowe shook his head. "I never thought I'd need the army to stand guard over my farm," he said.

"That's how it has to be until this thing is settled," the general replied. "Now then—how did the money get here?"

Quentin hardly heard the question. He was still thinking about Roselynn and Vincent and how angry they'd been when their money came back to the field. And they thought *he* was to blame. He felt his eyes sting with tears, and he wondered if he'd ever be friends with them again.

"Answer the man, son," said Poppa.

"I wished for it," Quentin said sadly. "And Flan

gave me my wish. All the money in the world."

"Oh, surely not that much," said the general. "Still, there's a lot of money out there. But you can't keep it, you know."

"Why not, sir . . . I mean, General? It's mine, isn't it?"

"Yours?" boomed the general. "Of course it's not yours. Let me tell you something, Quentin. That money . . ."

"Just a minute, General Mainwaring." Mr. Stowe held up a hand, and the general sputtered into silence.

"Quentin?" Mr. Stowe's voice was soft and gentle.

"Yes, Poppa?"

"Have you thought of where all that money came from?"

Quentin looked from Poppa to General Mainwaring and back again. "From all over," he said. "From banks and cities and . . ."

"And from people, Quentin. That money came right out of people's pockets. And I'm one of them. Right now, if the general offered to sell me his car for five cents, I wouldn't be able to buy it. Because my money's out in the fields with all the rest."

Slowly Quentin turned toward Flan, who was in the high chair, gobbling down his pie. "Is . . . is that right, Flan?"

The little man nodded. "If you'd asked for a few thousand dollars," he said, "I could have taken coins and bills that people had lost. Nobody would be the wiser. But you wanted all the money in the world. So the rich men had their wealth taken away. But so did the beggars who only had a few coins in their pockets."

"Then I stole . . ." Quentin began.

"Stealing's a harsh word," said Poppa. "You made a wish, Quentin. The way any boy might do. The difference is, you got what you wished for."

Quentin thought about this. He imagined people going hungry because their last bit of money had disappeared. He didn't want that to happen.

But he also thought about what he could do with all the money in the world. Bikes and ball gloves and fishing poles and candy and . . .

And people would be starving because he had their money.

"Why can't they just get along without money?" he shouted suddenly. Tears stung his eyes.

"Quentin," said Poppa, patting his arm gently. "Money isn't something just to have. It's something you use. It . . . well, I guess you might call it a way of keeping score."

"Keeping score, Poppa?"

"Let me put it this way. Suppose I hired General Mainwaring to work for me here. On the farm."

"Harrumph!" The general looked sternly at Mr. Stowe. But he didn't say a word. Poppa went on.

"All right, so I agree to pay him three dollars an hour. He works for me four hours. How much would I have to give him?"

"Twelve dollars," Quentin replied.

"Good." Poppa smiled. "But those twelve dollars are just a mess of paper. What do they stand for? How much work are they worth?"

Money? A mess of paper? It was hard to understand. "Four hours," he said.

"After work," said Poppa, "General Mainwaring decides to go into town. He figures on buying a shirt. In Hobson's Clothing Store, he finds just what he wants. A nice red shirt with stripes running down it. The price is six dollars. So the general gives Mr. Hobson six of those pieces of paper I paid him for his work, and in return, Mr. Hobson gives him the shirt."

"Yes, Poppa."

"Now let me ask you, Quentin. How much of the general's work is that shirt worth? At three dollars an hour?"

"Hmm. Two hours," said Quentin with a grin.

"Right." Poppa grinned back at him. "The general is saying that he'll swap two hours of his work for one shirt."

"But you said the general was working for you,"

said Quentin. "Not Mr. Hobson."

"True, Quentin. But maybe in a few days, Mr. Hobson decides he wants a few eggs and some fresh vegetables. He comes out here to buy them. Six dollars' worth. He uses the money the general gave him. So he's really paying for his food with two hours of the general's work. That's what I mean when I say the money is just used to keep score."

Money—money stood for work and food and clothes and . . . and all kinds of things! It was a new idea. Quentin needed time to think.

"But why don't people just trade for what they need?" he asked.

"Suppose the general wanted that shirt, but Mr. Hobson didn't have any work for him to do?" asked Poppa. "What then?"

"Couldn't you write a note, Poppa? Saying the general had worked for you, and you'd give Mr. Hobson food in trade for the shirt?"

"I could." Poppa smiled down at him. "And do you know what that note would be called?"

Suddenly, Quentin knew. "Money," he said.

So it wasn't just gold and paper and coins out there in the fields. It was all the wheat harvests in Kansas, and the steel out of Pittsburgh, and a chef preparing a fine meal, and a worker making machinery and . . . and . . . Quentin's eyes grew wide as he realized what all the money in the world stood for.

"I . . . I have to give it back, don't I?" he asked his father sadly.

"Yes, Quentin."

General Mainwaring's chair scraped against the floor. "That's easier said than done."

"What do you mean?" asked Mr. Stowe.

"The money. It seems to come back."

"Come back?" Mr. Stowe couldn't believe his ears.

"That's right. We tried loading some of it onto our trucks. But the minute the money got to the road, it came right back to your fields. Like it was homesick and wanted to get back with the rest of the money."

At this, Flan gave a shrill laugh.

"Homesick money!" he cackled. "That's good, General. That's very good. That's exactly what it is."

"Don't make fun of me, you little green . . ." General Mainwaring's hand moved toward the pistol at his belt.

"I wouldn't, if I were you," said Flan. "Remember the lobster, General."

The general's hand returned to the table.

"What's this all about, Flan?" asked Mr. Stowe.

"Think, sir. Think," the little man replied.

"What is there about the edge of the road that makes it special?"

"It's the border of my farm, that's all," said Mr. Stowe.

"Exactly," answered Flan. He turned to Quentin.

"Before you made your wish, lad, I said you had to be careful about something. Do you recall?"

Quentin thought back. "You told me whatever I wished for," he said slowly, "that I'd have it for all time."

Flan giggled. "That's it exactly."

"That's what, exactly?" roared General Mainwaring.

"General, sir, Quentin wished for all the money in the world. That was the bargain. And that's what he's to have. For as long as he lives.

"But if the soldiers took away some of the money . . ." Mr. Stowe began.

". . . Then Quentin would no longer have all the money in the world!" Flan hooted. "Our bargain would be broken. And the Law of the Leprechauns couldn't allow that to happen."

"But that means . . ." General Mainwaring gaped at the little man. "It means the money has to stay here. All of it. None of it can ever be taken away."

"That's right. Quentin made his wish. Now he's stuck with it."

"But that means even *I* can't take it away!" Quentin wailed.

"That's *your* problem," said Flan. "Not mine."

For a moment everyone was too amazed to speak. Finally Mr. Stowe leaned toward the little man.

"Could Quentin wish the money back where it belongs?" he asked.

Flan shook his head. "Not likely, sir. You see, he used up his last wish for the money. He has none left to wish it back again."

Mr. Stowe looked blankly at General Mainwaring.

General Mainwaring looked just as blankly at Mr. Stowe.

With a rush Quentin got up from the table. He ran up the stairs and into his room, slamming the door behind him. He didn't want Poppa to see the tears that were streaming down his cheeks.

He threw himself onto the bed and buried his face in the pillow.

It just wasn't fair. People all over the world were suffering because they had no money. And he had all the money in the world, but he couldn't do anything with it. It would just sit out there on the farm, killing all the crops and damming up the creek to the pasture so he and Poppa would have to carry water to the animals every single morning and every single afternoon for the rest of their lives.

No new bike, no baseball glove, no candy.

No more Roselynn and Vincent.

No nothing.

Just a lot of hard work. Harder than before.

It wasn't fair.

# 7
# *The Only Shopper in Town*

The following morning, after he'd carried water for the animals, Quentin stood at the edge of the road, looking forlornly at the vast fields of money. Nearby, there was a rustling of bills, and then Flan's voice:

"There you are, woodchuck. I see your tail behind those dimes. One, two, three, you're caught, and I win."

A whole farm piled high with money. And that's all it was good for—playing games. Nobody—not even Quentin—could take it and use it. And because of it, in addition to his other troubles, Roselynn and Vincent weren't his friends anymore.

Idly he picked up a stack of ten-dollar bills in his right hand. His left hand gripped a roll of quarters, and he stood weighing the coins against the bills.

"Good morning, Quentin!"

Startled, Quentin jammed the money into his pockets and looked around.

"Good morning!" called the voice again. Across the road at the army camp, one of the soldiers was waving at him. It was the sergeant who had looked so stern yesterday. But now he was smiling.

"Good morning," Quentin answered.

The sergeant walked across the road, holding out a tin plate of scrambled eggs. "Would you like some breakfast?"

"No, I already ate."

"You must get up pretty early."

"Poppa and I had to water the animals," said Quentin. "This afternoon we'll have to do it again. And all because of the money."

"Yes, it's really made a mess of your farm. How much do you suppose there is?"

"It's all the money in the world."

The sergeant chuckled. He didn't believe Quentin.

"And now I've got it all, and my best friends won't even play with me," Quentin went on. "I gave them some, but . . . well, you saw what happened."

"Yeah," said the sergeant. "The money came back when they left the farm, and they got mad at you." He patted Quentin's shoulder comfortingly.

"Would it help if I was your friend?" he asked Quentin. "I'm Sergeant Tucker to the army, but my friends call me Ray. How does that sound to you?"

"Ray?" Quentin felt good when he said it. "Yeah, that's okay." It was the first time a grown-up had let him use a first name. Here he was, talking to a real soldier and calling him Ray.

"Sergeant Tucker!" called the lieutenant from the camp across the road. "Line up the men!"

"Yes, sir!" Quentin was startled by Ray's loud answer. It was so different from the way he had sounded a minute ago.

"Awright, everybody out! Awright, awright, let's go!"

Ray turned and winked at Quentin. "Come down and see me after supper tonight," he said. "I'll show you what a real army camp looks like."

As Ray walked away, Quentin could see men running about in the camp, putting on helmets and looking at their rifles. A few soldiers were guarding some trucks parked at the side of the road. Quentin put Flan up on his shoulder. Then he climbed the fence and walked across the road toward them.

One of the soldiers pointed at Flan. "Is that the little green man I've been hearing about?" he asked.

"Yes, sir." As Quentin came closer to the trucks

he kept one eye on the guards.

"Go ahead," said one of them. "Take a good look. Climb behind the wheel."

Quentin got into the truck. He sat down, put Flan on the seat beside him, and pretended he was driving. Then he got out again.

The day was getting hot. Where the sun hit the road, the tar was sticky under Quentin's shoes.

The road!

Quentin crammed his hands into his pockets.

The bills and the roll of quarters were still there! They hadn't gone back to the farm!

Slowly he walked around the truck, expecting at every step that his money would vanish. But the wad of bills and the roll of quarters stayed in his pockets.

Somehow the spell of the homesick money must have been broken.

"Flan!" he called. "Flan, come on!"

The little man was still bouncing on the seat of the truck. "Yes, Quentin," he said. "What is it?"

"I'll get my bike. Then we're going into town."

"Will I see Mrs. Trussker?" Flan asked fearfully. "I don't think I could stand another dose of her singing."

"We won't go anywhere near her house. Come on. We'll have some fun."

Pedaling into town with Flan lying in the basket

of the bike, Quentin kept patting the money in his pockets. Money to spend. Any way he wanted to. Wonderful!

He coasted down the long hill that led to the business area of Cedar Ferry.

Then he came to a stop.

The stores on both sides of Main Street seemed to be open. A dog chased a cat across the road. And somewhere he could hear the sound of a man chopping wood.

But that was all. Something was wrong.

In the middle of the morning there should have been people in the stores and walking along the sidewalk. But as far as Quentin could see, he was the only shopper in town.

"Where is everybody?" he exclaimed.

"Probably at home," said Flan. "As you have all the money in the world, what reason would they have to come to the stores?"

"Oh." Quentin rubbed his fingers against the money in his pocket.

He leaned his bike against the wall of a small store on the left side of the street. A sign above the door had a few letters missing. It read:

WALT MILLERIDGE
IC      REAM

Some of the letters had been blown off in a storm, but Mr. Milleridge still made the best ice cream Quentin had ever tasted.

When he walked into the store a little bell above the door jingled. At the same time he could hear a voice from a TV somewhere in the back.

"It's now certain that there is no money at all in any bank, business, or home in the United States. We also have reports from several countries in Europe that their money supply has . . ."

The TV was switched off. Then Mr. Milleridge came out of the back room, wiping his hands on a towel.

"Oh, it's you, Quentin Stowe," he said with a scowl. "Maybe you hadn't heard, but I'm quitting the ice-cream business. And it's your fault, too. Folks can't buy ice cream as long as you've got all their money out there on your farm.

"And don't go asking for credit, either," he went on. "Some of the soldiers from that camp came in here last evening. They said that money keeps coming back to you. It'll probably stay on your Pa's place forever. So you'll be getting no ice cream or anything else from . . ."

And then he stopped talking and stood blinking at Flan, who sat on one of the stools with his head just peeping over the edge of the counter.

"He's green, ain't he?"

"Yes," said Quentin.

"Little bit of a thing, ain't he?"

Quentin nodded. "But he's over three hundred years old."

"I see," said Mr. Milleridge. "I guess lots of things would turn green after three hundred years."

Flan grabbed a pack of chewing gum from a little box on the counter. "Can I have this, Quentin?"

"Sure. But remember to take the paper off before you put it in your mouth."

"Just a minute." Mr. Milleridge glared down at Quentin and Flan. "I thought I made it clear you get nothing from me without the money to pay for it."

"Oh, I have plenty of money." Quentin took the roll of quarters from his pocket and banged it on the counter. He tore open the end of the roll, and five coins rolled out.

"That's money!" Mr. Milleridge stared at the coins as if they were diamonds. He picked one up and bit it between his teeth. "Real money," he sighed.

He wiped the counter with a cloth and smiled at Quentin. "What'll it be?"

"I'll have a chocolate ice-cream soda and . . ." Quentin turned to Flan. "Do you want anything?"

"Uggh. Hmmzzz. Bffssl." The little man had crammed the whole pack of gum into his mouth. His cheek bulged out in a big green lump. It was impossible for him to talk, but there was a big smile on his face.

"Just the soda," Quentin said. "And the gum, of course."

When Quentin had finished the soda, Mr. Milleridge held out his hand greedily. "That'll be eighty-five cents."

Eighty-five cents. Well, three quarters made seventy-five cents, and four quarters were a dollar. Quentin put four quarters on the counter.

"Change, please," he said.

"Change? I haven't got any change. Nobody has any money at all. Except you."

"Then can I give you seventy-five cents and owe you the extra dime?"

"I've got a better idea," Mr. Milleridge answered. "Suppose you give me four of those quarters, and I'll owe you fifteen cents."

Quentin didn't think that was a better idea at all. But then he laughed. What was fifteen cents to him? He had all the money in the world.

"Okay, Mr. Milleridge."

The next stop was Hobson's Clothing Store. Mrs. Hobson was sitting just inside the door, knitting a scarf.

"Good day, Quentin," she said coolly. "I didn't think you'd take time off from counting all your money to come visiting."

"I'm not here for a visit," Quentin replied. "I want to buy Momma a nice coat for when it turns cold."

"We have coats, right enough," said Mrs. Hobson with a toss of her head. "And you certainly have the money. But getting your money down here to our store—that's the problem, isn't it?"

Without a word Quentin took out the stack of ten-dollar bills and showed it to her.

Mrs. Hobson shot out of her chair and rushed to the rear of the store. "Cory!" she called. "Cory Hobson, you get off that couch and come out here. Quentin Stowe's here with money—real money!"

Mr. Hobson dashed from the rear of the store, buttoning his shirt as he came. He took one of the bills and held it up to the light.

"It's genuine," he said.

*"EEEEK!"*

Mrs. Hobson had grabbed a broom from the corner and was pointing at something on the other side of the store.

"It's green, Cory!" she screeched. "Rats, that's it. We've got green rats!"

"That's just Flan," said Quentin. "He's green, but he's friendly."

Flan marched across the floor and made a low

bow to Mrs. Hobson. She held up the broom as if to swat him.

"Emma, cut that out," said Mr. Hobson. "If Quentin has real money to spend, what do we care who his friends are?"

He finally calmed his wife down, and with nervous looks at Flan, she helped Quentin pick out a fine coat for Momma. It was thick and warm, and it had a collar of real fur. It cost ninety-two dollars.

Quentin laid down ten of the ten-dollar bills to pay for it. This time he knew better than to ask for change.

The third shop was the jewelry store. Quentin picked out a gold watch for Poppa. The price was a hundred and twenty-three dollars.

"Do you want it in a gift box?" asked Miss Draymore, who owned the store.

Before Quentin could answer, the door of the shop burst open. Mr. Hobson rushed in, followed by his wife, who pointed a finger at Quentin.

"You!" she snapped in an angry voice. "You tricked us."

"Me? But . . . but . . ."

Before he could say anything more, Mr. Milleridge ran in and stood beside the Hobsons. He poked a finger toward Quentin's face.

"Where is it?" he roared. "My money—where is it?"

Miss Draymore was holding the watch in its

black box. "May I ask what's going on here?"

"He bought a soda in my store!" bellowed Mr. Milleridge. "And some gum. Paid for it with four quarters. At least I thought he did. I watched him and that green man walk outside, but when I turned around, the quarters were gone."

"And I was sure Quentin gave me the money for the coat he bought," added Mrs. Hobson. "But when I went to pick it up, it . . . it wasn't there anymore. Like it was magic money or something."

"Indeed," said Miss Draymore, primly. "Well there's certainly nothing wrong with the money I received from Quentin. Look, it's right here in the . . . the . . ." Miss Draymore blinked down at the drawer where she had placed the money for the watch.

"Empty!" she said, astonished.

"Here, give me that!" Mr. Hobson snatched back the coat box. "Play tricks, will you? You should be in jail, Quentin Stowe."

He and his wife marched out of the shop, mumbling angrily.

"Quentin," said Miss Draymore, "I'm afraid that the watch . . . well, I'll just have to put it back."

"And what about me?" said Mr. Milleridge. "How do I get my ice-cream soda back? And the gum?"

Quentin crammed his hands into his pockets,

grasping for money. In the left pocket was the opened roll of quarters and what was left of the stack of ten-dollar bills.

He reached into the right pocket. Uh-oh. Now it held money, too. Ten-dollar bills. He counted them. Twenty-three. Ten of them for the coat and thirteen more for the watch. Plus four quarters.

All the money he'd spent, back in his pockets again!

"Flan!" he yelled at the top of his voice. And at that moment he felt Mr. Milleridge's big hand grab the collar of his shirt.

Mr. Milleridge half led, half dragged Quentin to the storeroom in the basement of the ice-cream store. The place was a mess, with boxes, paper cups, glasses, and dishes strewn all over.

"You get this place cleaned up!" Mr. Milleridge roared. "If I'm satisfied with the job, we'll be even for the soda and the gum. But if I'm not, you'll do it all over again."

He left the room, slamming the door behind him.

"What happened, Flan?" Quentin asked the little man, who was sitting on a bag of sugar in one corner. "How come I can carry the money, but nobody else can have any?"

"It's as I said before, lad. The money's yours for all time. You can take it where you like, but if you

give it to somebody else, you won't have all the money in the world anymore. So it has to return to you."

"It's not right," Quentin complained, as he lifted a heavy tray of glasses from the floor onto a high shelf. Then he took a broom and began sweeping the floor.

"I came to town with a lot of money, and I was ready to spend it. And now I've got to clean this whole place just because I had an ice-cream soda. No soda in the world is that good."

It took him almost an hour to finish the job. His back ached, and his face and hair were covered with dust. Somehow he'd have to find the energy to pedal his bike back home. But once there, at least he'd be able to tumble right into bed.

But then he looked at the clock on the wall. "Oh, no!" he cried. For by the time he got home, it would be almost time to tote water for the animals again.

There was still plenty of daylight after supper that evening. Tired as he was, Quentin still wanted to visit Sergeant Ray Tucker at the army camp.

When he arrived, with Flan on his shoulder, the soldiers were in groups around small fires. Some of them were playing cards, and others were reading or just talking. Ray was in his tent, seated on the cot and polishing his shoes. "Would you like to see what the camp looks like?" he asked.

Quentin nodded quickly. Ray put on his shoes and then walked outside. "There's the mess tent," he said, pointing. "That's where we eat. The trucks are parked over there, and those other tents are where the men sleep."

"I thought there'd be cannons and tanks," said Quentin.

"We don't need them unless somebody tries to take away the money. And after what's happened, I don't think they'd get very far."

He stopped under a tree and looked down at Quentin. "How does it feel to have all that money?" he asked.

"Not very good." Quentin told Ray about his trip into town.

"It seems to me there's more bad things about having all this money than there are good ones," said Ray. "But if you could buy just one thing, Quentin, what would it be?"

"That's easy. A ten-speed bike. Just like Rose-lynn Peabody and Vincent Arbor have."

"They're those friends of yours?"

"They used to be."

"You know, I've got a daughter just about your

age. She wants a bike, too. I was going to get her one in a few days, but . . ."

"Why don't you?" Quentin asked.

"How?" Ray pulled his pockets inside out. "I don't have any money. None of the soldiers do. And it's hard getting them to obey orders when there's no money to pay them."

Quentin looked across the road at the heaps of money. He very much wanted it just to go away. "I . . . I guess I'd better be going," he said.

As he walked to the edge of the road, two other men in uniform came up to him.

"You're Quentin Stowe, aren't you?" one of them asked.

"Yes, sir."

"General Mainwaring would like a word with you. He's in the car there."

Quentin wondered what the general wanted. He followed after the two men.

When they reached the car, the smaller man opened the front door and got in. The other man opened the back door.

Quentin looked inside. There was nobody there.

"Where's General Mainwaring?" he asked loudly.

"Shut the kid up," ordered the small man. "We'll have the whole army over here."

The two men weren't soldiers at all!

Before Quentin could say or do anything, he was lifted up and thrown onto the rear seat. Flan came tumbling in on top of him. Quentin opened his mouth to shout.

But the bigger man put a handkerchief over his face.

Quentin smelled something that reminded him of hospitals and doctors. Then his head started to spin, and his eyes began to close. He tried to get up, but the man was much stronger than he was. And he was sleepy . . . so sleepy. . . .

With a loud roar, the car sped off down the road. But Quentin didn't hear the car.

He couldn't hear anything.

# 8
# Kidnapped

When Quentin finally opened his eyes, he was lying on a hard wooden floor. He tried to sit up, but the bare walls of the little room seemed to spin, first one way and then the other. Next to him, Flan was sitting cross-legged, puffing contentedly on his pipe.

The building was a small hut or shack. The two men were sitting at a table in the center of it. They weren't wearing the uniforms anymore. There were newspapers, paste, and scissors on the table, as well as an oil lamp. The shadows made on the walls by the lamp were large and spooky.

The big man nudged his friend. "The kid's awake."

"Well, go tie him up," replied the smaller man. "That green thing, too."

"I don't like this." The big man shook his head. "The green guy keeps looking at me awful strange."

They'd been kidnapped! Quentin was scared. Suppose the men just left him here? How would he ever get back home?

But Flan looked up calmly as the big man came over to them. "And what were you going to use to tie us with?" he asked.

"This rope, that's what," said the man.

"What rope?" Flan waved his hand through the air. "I don't see any rope."

"This rope I got here in my . . ." The man stopped and stared at what he held in his hand. It wasn't rope, but coil after coil of paper ribbon in bright reds and yellows and blues.

"Oh, good." Flan chuckled. "A party. We'll all make paper chains. What fun!"

The big man threw the strips of paper into a corner. "Grundy!" he howled. "It ain't rope anymore. It's paper!"

97

The smaller kidnapper was busy at the table. "Keep quiet," he said without looking up. "I told you to get rope. If you made a mistake, that's your problem. And stop using my name. Do you want them to know who we are?"

"Right, Grundy. I won't tell 'em your name anymore, Grundy."

The man at the table covered his face with his hands and sighed. "Edgar, you are the world's most stupid kidnapper."

"He really likes me," said Edgar to Quentin. "Grundy just talks that way sometimes. Now don't either of you move, or I'll have to hurt you."

"We'll do whatever you say," said Flan with a twinkle in his eye, "if you'll just give us something to eat. I'm hungry."

Edgar got a can of beans from a box in one corner. He opened the can and gave it to Quentin.

"You can share the beans," he said. "But no fair moving. You promised."

"Edgar," called Grundy. "Come over here. I need help with this ransom note."

Edgar went back to the table. Flan shoveled a spoonful of beans into his mouth and handed the can to Quentin.

"What . . . what are they going to do to us?" Quentin asked.

"They won't harm you, lad," replied Flan. "I'll see to that."

Grundy was muttering to Edgar. "Now I've got all the words for the ransom note cut out of the newspapers. I'll hand each one to you, and you paste it down on this sheet of paper. Got it?"

"Got it," said Edgar happily. "Gee, what a good game."

"It's not a game," snapped Grundy. "When the note is finished, we leave it at the boy's house. Okay, here's the first word."

Silently Grundy passed Edgar one bit of newspaper after another. Edgar pasted each one in place, pounding it loudly with his hand to flatten it.

"Okay, let's see what you've got so far," Grundy said finally.

He took the paper and held it in the light. Over his shoulder Quentin could see the bits of newspaper. But they didn't seem to make much sense.

**IG SALE TODA** ashington **ee-base hi**

WANT ADS **$4**⁹⁵
                amous Hollywood actr

**MONEY DISAPPEA** flat feet?

Grundy let out a howl. Edgar looked at him. "I pasted the things all down, just the way you said," he pouted.

"Sure you did. Only the message was supposed to read: WE HAVE YOUR BOY. TO GET HIM BACK . . . And that's as far as I'd gone."

Edgar squinted at the paper. "That's not what it says here, Grundy."

"Of course not, you dope. We needed the words that were on the *other* side of the paper—the side you put the paste on!"

Grundy got up and walked over to Quentin and Flan. "Do you know why you're here, kid?" he asked.

"I . . . I think so, Mr. Grundy. I think you want . . ."

"Money! That's what we want. We heard about all that money piled up on your farm."

"I've got all the money in the world," said Quentin proudly. But when he saw the look in Grundy's eye, he wished he hadn't said it.

Grundy gave a low whistle and turned to Edgar. "When you do that note again," he said, "tell his parents we're asking for one million dollars."

"Right, Grundy." Edgar began searching through the newspapers for the figure $1,000,000.

One million dollars! Quentin wondered how big a pile one million dollars would make.

And then he remembered something.

"Mr. Grundy," he said softly.

"Yeah, kid?"

"If you'll just let us go, I'll give you money. All you want."

"Oh?" Grundy was definitely interested.

"Yes, sir. Just bring your car to the money field. You can fill it with money."

"We'll even help you load it," Flan added with an impish grin.

Grundy couldn't believe his ears. He looked down at Quentin. "Is this some kind of a trick?"

"I want to go home," Quentin replied. "And on that farm is all the money in the world. Even after you fill your car, there will still be plenty left."

"But what about the soldiers?"

"They won't hurt you. They may even help."

"Well . . ." Grundy thought about this. "I hope you wouldn't lie to us. It would be too dangerous for you."

Five minutes later Edgar was driving toward the money field. Grundy bounced around in the back-seat of the car with Quentin and Flan.

"Remember," Grundy said. "One false move and we're going to have to hurt you." He squeezed Quentin's arm hard.

"Ow!" cried Quentin. "We won't try anything."

When they reached the farm, Edgar parked the car right up on the grass near the fence. "The gold," he said. "Let's get the gold, Grundy. And some bills. Twenties and fifties and . . ."

"I'll take care of the money. You just keep the car running so we can get away fast if we have to."

Edgar stayed in the car while Grundy, Quentin, and Flan climbed over the fence. "We'll each carry one bag of gold coins back first," Grundy whispered.

They staggered back to the car and put the heavy bags into the trunk. They were just ready to go back for more when Grundy put his finger to his lips.

"There's a man across the road," he said softly. "Looks like a soldier."

"Quentin, is that you?"

It was Sergeant Ray Tucker.

"Just keep quiet," Grundy whispered. But Ray began walking toward them.

"Hi, Quentin," he said. "You'd better be getting home. Your parents were down here asking about you."

"I'll see he gets home," said Grundy. He had a tight grip on Quentin's shoulder.

"Who's this?" Ray asked.

"It's a friend of mine," Quentin answered. He didn't want the kidnappers to hurt anybody. "I told him he could take some money from the field."

"You told him *what*? Quentin, you know the money . . ."

"Ray!" Quentin said loudly. "It's my money, and I can give it to anybody I want to."

"Yeah, Quentin. Sure." Ray didn't know what was going on. Grundy's grip on Quentin's shoulder loosened.

"Will you help us load the car, Ray?"

"All right. If that's what you want."

With Ray's help, the car was soon weighted down with coins and bills and gold. Grundy got in beside Edgar.

Quentin, Flan, and Ray stood at the edge of the road. "That money is ransom, isn't it?" Ray asked quietly. "Those men kidnapped you."

Quentin nodded.

"I'll call my men," Ray went on. "Let's capture them."

"No," said Quentin. "They really aren't very good kidnappers. And they didn't hurt us."

Grundy started the car. Its wheels rolled out onto the road.

*Pong!*

The car bounced twice and then screeched to a stop. Edgar looked in the backseat. Then he got out and opened the trunk.

"The money, Grundy!" he shouted. "It's gone!"

"It can't be." Grundy got out and looked into the trunk. "But it is."

He pointed a finger at Quentin. "All right, you

and your friends load the car again.

"Come on," Quentin said to Ray. "It's good exercise."

Again the car was backed up to the fence and loaded with money. Grundy locked the back doors and tied the trunk down with a piece of rope.

Edgar steered the car onto the road.

*Pong!*

Grundy looked very frightened. "What's going on here?" he asked.

"The money's got a magic spell on it." Quentin giggled. "It can't leave the field."

"Impossible!" Grundy screeched. He shook his head. "You really mean we can't take it off the farm?"

"That's right, Mr. Grundy."

"I told that dumb Edgar we should just rob a bank," Grundy said. "But no. He wanted to try kidnapping."

Edgar came running up. "What happened?" he asked.

Grundy told him. "Next time, we rob a bank," he finished.

"That won't do you any good either," said Ray with a laugh.

"Why not?"

"The banks don't have any money. It's all here."

"Oh." Together the two men trudged sadly toward their car. Grundy's last words drifted back to Quentin.

"It's awful, Edgar. I guess we're going to have to do some honest work for a change."

When Quentin got back to the house, Momma gave him a big hug. "Where have you been?" she asked in a worried tone.

Then she got all angry and shook him by the shoulder. "You know better than to stay out this late, Quentin Stowe!"

When Quentin told her about the kidnapping, she was very frightened. But both she and Poppa laughed when he got to the part about the disappearing money.

"You have to stay awake a little longer," said Momma. "Go in the living room, both of you. I'll get us something to eat."

Quentin looked up at Poppa. "What's going on?"

"The President is going to be on TV again," answered Poppa. "In just a few minutes. We of all people should hear what he has to say."

Ten minutes later Quentin was curled up on the sofa, munching a cookie and watching the President on the TV screen.

"Today," the President said, "I met with my economic advisors, businessmen, and representatives from several European countries. I have been informed that these countries have had their money vanish, too.

"The situation is so desperate that people can no longer buy food, clothing, and the other things they need to stay alive. But there is even more to it than that.

"Banks throughout the world have had to close. And business and industry cannot continue to operate. To be brief, unless some way can be found to restore our money supply, life for all of us will become very grim indeed."

Quentin looked from Momma to Poppa. They were both staring at the TV screen with worried looks on their faces.

"But there is still hope," the President went on. "I have received word that a large part of the money—perhaps all of it—has been located. And while the army has the money under guard, its location must be kept secret. At least until certain problems concerning the return of the money can be solved."

"He's talking about this place—this farm!" gasped Momma.

"Shh!" Poppa hissed. "Let him finish."

"In conclusion," said the President, "I ask for the help and cooperation of every citizen of this great country. Each city . . . each town . . . each village . . . must find its own way of providing the goods and services we all need so much. At this time, when there is no money, we must depend on the help, kindness, and goodwill of one another if we are to survive."

The President bowed his head. Then the TV screen went blank.

"Oh, George," said Momma. "We've got to do *something*. The President himself asked us."

"But there isn't anything we haven't . . ." Before Poppa could finish, the telephone rang.

Poppa answered it. Quentin heard just a few words.

"Yes, Roscoe. . . . Tomorrow? Of course. . . . We'll have to think of something. . . . Yes, I'll make sure he's there. . . . Good-bye, Roscoe."

He hung up the receiver. Then he looked across the room at Quentin.

"Bedtime for you," Poppa said. "You've got a big day ahead of you."

"What do you mean, Poppa?"

"Mayor Peabody's calling a town meeting at the Cedar Ferry firehouse," said Poppa. "We're all going to do just what the President asked. There has to be some way of getting Cedar Ferry running again, money or no money."

"But why do I have to go?" Quentin asked.

"Why, you're the guest of honor," said Poppa with a little smile. "With all that money out back, you're the most important person in the whole world."

# 9
# Cedar Ferry Town Meeting

Almost all the grown-ups in Cedar Ferry were waiting inside the Volunteer Fire Department when the Stowes arrived. There were cars parked all over the streets, and the Stowes could hear an angry rumbling of voices from inside.

They walked up the front steps, and Mayor Roscoe Peabody greeted them.

"Good afternoon, Mr. and Mrs. Stowe. Hello, Quentin. I see Flan decided to come, too."

Flan, perched on Quentin's shoulder, waved to the mayor.

"Why aren't you inside with the rest?" Mr. Stowe asked.

"Well, I like to shake hands with folks coming in. And besides, I want to make sure nobody trips over this rotten place in the steps."

Near the mayor's feet, Quentin could see a place on the steps where the paint was peeling and the wood was wet and soft.

"We've got to fix that," said the mayor. "Just as soon as there's money to do it." He looked sternly at Quentin and Flan.

Inside, Quentin sat between his parents on a

bench at the back of the large room. Mayor Peabody stood at the speaker's table and rapped for order with a big wooden hammer.

"We'll start off," he said, "with Mrs. Viola Trussker singing 'The Star-Spangled Banner.'"

Mrs. Trussker came to the front of the room. Everybody stood up.

*"Oh say, can you see . . ."*

Flan clapped his hands over his ears and crawled under the bench. "A fine song," he whispered to Quentin. "Why must she hoot it out like a dying loon? It's more than a body can bear."

Finally the song was finished, and the people sat down.

"You folks all heard the President on the TV yesterday," the mayor began. "As long as we can't get any money, it's up to us to keep Cedar Ferry running properly without it. The question is—how are we going to do that?"

"Quentin Stowe's got all that money out on his farm," a woman called out. "I'd paddle his britches if he doesn't give it back."

"Why don't we just go out there and take it?" shouted someone. "I don't believe all that stuff about how it keeps coming back to the farm. And if there were enough of us, the Stowes wouldn't dare stop us."

Angry voices were heard all over the room.

110

Quentin began to tremble. He looked up at Poppa.

Mr. Stowe stood up. "That's enough!" he said angrily. The people became silent.

"The money's out on my farm, and if anybody can take it away, he'd be thanked by me and my family. But I guess you've heard, we're having trouble getting it off the fields." Poppa shook his head in wonderment. "It keeps coming back."

"You mean it'll be there forever?" Emma Hobson called out.

"You'd better ask Flan about that," replied Mr. Stowe. He bent down, picked up the little man, and held him up for everybody to see.

"Flan," said Mayor Peabody, "is what Mr. Stowe says true?"

"It is," Flan answered. "I gave Quentin just what he wished for."

"But if you brought the money, you must be able to return it."

Flan shook his head. "I cannot take back a wish once it's been granted. That's the Law of the Leprechauns."

"I say we put the green man in jail until he agrees to return the money," said Walt Milleridge.

"We can't do it," replied Sheriff Arbor. "He walks through walls."

"And if you try any rough stuff," Flan squeaked, "I'll turn the lot of you into mud turtles."

"I think he could do it, too, folks," added Mayor Peabody.

The room was silent. The people looked at one another in surprise. Then a man in one corner got to his feet.

"Some of us have made a plan about the money problem, at least here in Cedar Ferry," he said. "We think it'll work, for the time being." He and a second man picked up a large box and carried it to the front of the room.

"Folks," said Mayor Peabody, "you all know Bob Reese who owns the variety store. And Joe Ballard, the butcher. Tell 'em your plan, fellows."

Bob Reese reached down into the box. He pulled out and held up something that looked to Quentin very much like a stack of bills from one of the piles on the farm. But how could money be here?

"I've got four boxes of this down in the basement of my store," said Mr. Reese. "It's play money."

He pulled one of the bills from the stack. "Instead of a dollar, this is called a 'dilly.' There are bills in this box marked one, five, ten, and twenty dillies. And it's our plan to turn this play money into real money."

"How?" asked Mayor Peabody.

"We all know about how much everybody in town earns. So we'd give everybody here a week's wages, right now. Only it'd be in dillies, not dollars. But we'd all agree that here in Cedar Ferry, we'd spend and receive the dillies just like real money."

"That sounds reasonable," said a man.

"And it'd help our businesses to get started again," added a woman.

"Mr. Reese?" Miss Draymore, who ran the jewelry store, got to her feet. "Your plan sounds well and good, as far as it goes. But what would happen if somebody found another supply of those . . . those dillies? Someone could come in here from another village with a pocketful of dillies and begin spending them. We'd never know the difference. We'd just have a lot of dillies that weren't worth anything."

"We already thought of that," said Joe Ballard. From the pocket of his butcher's apron he pulled out a rubber stamp. He pressed the stamp against one of the dilly bills.

Bob Reese held the bill up for all to see. Stamped across its front in red letters were the words COLD CUTS.

"Our plan," Mr. Ballard went on, "is to stamp each bill with my COLD CUTS stamp. They would be the only official money in Cedar Ferry. Any bills that didn't have the stamp would be bad money, and Sheriff Arbor would arrest anybody who tried to spend it."

114

"And who'd guard the rubber stamp itself?" asked Miss Draymore.

"It would be kept in a locked box at the bank," said Mr. Ballard. "Mayor Peabody would have the key. But even he couldn't get the stamp unless Banker Sedgewick led him to the box."

Miss Draymore thought about this. "That seems safe enough," she said finally. There were murmurs of agreement from around the room.

"Then let's get going," ordered the mayor. "I call on Mr. Ballard, Mr. Reese, and Miss Draymore to start stamping all the dilly bills in this box. And Sheriff Arbor, you keep an eye on them to see that they do it right."

Mr. Reese spread the bills out on the table. Mr. Ballard took an ink pad from his pocket, and Miss Draymore started stamping each bill. Thump, thump, thump. She moved the stamp faster than the eye could follow.

Finally all the bills were printed with the COLD CUTS stamp. They were all put back into the big box.

"Now I want everybody who earns money to get into a line," ordered the mayor. "Each one will come up and say how much you earn in a week. Banker Sedgewick will sit at the table here. If what you tell him sounds about right, he'll give you that much in dillies. Let's start with you, Dr. Snow."

Dr. Snow was short, with white hair. "It's hard to tell," he said. "Some weeks I have a lot of patients, and other times there aren't very many. I'd say about three hundred dollars, though."

Banker Sedgewick slid three hundred dollars in dilly bills across the table.

The second man was Wilber Vickers, who did odd jobs in Cedar Ferry. He asked for seventy-five dollars.

"It doesn't seem right," he said. "Dr. Snow gets three hundred dollars, and I get seventy-five."

"Lots of people can mow lawns and shovel snow," said Mayor Peabody. "It takes a lot of school to become a doctor."

For nearly an hour people went to the table to get money. When it was his turn, Mr. Stowe asked for ninety dollars. He received four twenty-dilly bills and a ten-dilly bill. "There's just about enough here to buy me a suit of clothes," he said to Quentin as he sat down.

When everyone had his dillies, Mayor Peabody rapped the table for quiet. "Is everybody satisfied?" he called out.

"No, I'm not." Wilber Vickers stood up.

"What's the matter, Wilber?" asked the mayor.

"I was thinking just last week about raising my prices for mowing lawns and cleaning windows," said Mr. Vickers. "You remember, Mr.

Sedgewick. I spoke to you about it."

Banker Sedgewick nodded. "That's true. Maybe we should have given him more money, Mr. Peabody."

"Okay, Wilber," said the mayor. "Will another twenty-five dillies be all right?"

"Fine." Mr. Vickers came forward and took the extra dillies.

"Hey, Wilber cleans the windows of my store," called out Mr. Hobson. "If I pay him more, I'll have to raise my prices. I should get more money, too."

"And me!" shouted Walt Milleridge.

"And me!"

"And me!"

Soon people were calling out all over the room. And one person after another came up to get more dillies.

By the time Mr. Stowe reached the table, the dillies were nearly gone. But he collected fifty more one-dilly bills.

"Isn't it wonderful, Poppa?" said Quentin. "Now, instead of ninety dillies, you've got a hundred and forty."

But Mr. Stowe didn't seem very happy. He whispered to Mr. Hobson.

"How much do you want for that brown suit in your window? The one you were going to sell for ninety dollars?"

"You know, I've got to raise the price because now I'll have to pay Wilber Vickers and others more for the things I want," said Mr. Hobson. "I can let you have it for a hundred and fifty dillies. No, you're a good customer. I'll take something off the price. It will cost you only a hundred and forty dillies."

Mr. Stowe looked at the money in his hands. "First I had ninety dillies," he said softly. "Now I've got a hundred and forty. But both times, I've only got enough to buy me that same new suit."

"If anybody's got debts to pay off," the mayor called out, "now would be a good time to do it. The whole town is here, and we all have money."

There was a rustling of bills and the sound of low voices.

"Now we're all settled up."

"I'll pay you the rest when I get paid."

"You still owe . . ."

And then, as if out of nowhere, a little pile of dilly bills appeared in Quentin's lap.

The pile grew larger . . . and larger . . . and larger. Finally Quentin was almost buried beneath the huge mound of dilly bills.

"Hey, look. The money disappeared."

"What happened to it?"

"Over there in the back. See?"

"Young Quentin Stowe has all our money."

"How did that happen?"

"I don't know. But let's get it back."

All over the room, people began getting up. They began to crowd toward Quentin.

Flan scurried among their legs and got to the speaker's table. He climbed up on it and spread his arms wide.

"You fools!" he cried. "Don't you see what's happened?"

"What?" asked the mayor. "What's happened?"

The mob of people turned to listen.

"The dilly bills were fake money," said Flan. "But now you're using them to buy and sell things."

"Sure," said someone. "Because now they're real money."

"Exactly," said Flan. "And since they're real money, Quentin gets them. Because now they're part of all the money in the world."

"We . . . we can't use them?" the mayor sputtered.

"Let's take 'em back!" shouted Emma Hobson.

"Right. They really belong to us, don't they?"

"Get that money!"

The crowd turned once more toward the bench where Quentin was sitting under the pile of dilly bills.

"Run, Quentin," said Mr. Stowe. "Get outside.

I'll try to stop them as long as I can. Ruth, you go with him."

"No," said Mrs. Stowe. "I'll stay here and help you, George."

Before Quentin himself could decide what to do, the door at the back of the room burst open.

There stood General Mainwaring, with his lieutenant beside him.

"Quentin Stowe," said the general. "Is he here?"

"Right there," growled someone, pointing at the mound of bills.

"Good." The general reached into the pile of dillies and took Quentin by the arm. "You're coming with me."

"But why?" Quentin asked.

"Because," said the general in a deep voice, "you have an appointment to keep. An appointment with the President of the United States."

## 10
# 1600 Pennsylvania Avenue

Quentin and Flan looked through the window at the buildings far below. Behind them Momma was saying something to Poppa, but over the loud *whap—whap—whap* of the helicopter blades,

Quentin couldn't hear what they were talking about.

His head was still spinning. Less than two hours ago he had been sitting in the Cedar Ferry Volunteer Fire Department with dilly bills all about him. Then General Mainwaring had whisked him and Momma and Poppa and Flan to an airport where a jet plane was waiting. The plane had flown high above the clouds, and when it came down they were all in Washington, D.C.

A special helicopter was waiting for them. It carried them straight up and zoomed across the city toward 1600 Pennsylvania Avenue—the White House, where the President lived.

General Mainwaring leaned across his seat. "That long building with the dome is the Capitol, Quentin," he said. "And look. We're going right by the top of the Washington Monument."

"Wow!" Quentin looked down. It was like a great stone needle pointing high into the air, and the top of it seemed almost close enough to reach out and touch.

"And there's the White House."

Quentin saw a big green area, with trees and flowers all around. In its center was the White House. It was huge, with rows of windows stretching away from the curved porch in the center. The pillars of the porch reminded him of pictures of old buildings in his history books. It all looked so grand that he could hardly wait to see it up close.

The helicopter landed softly, and the blades whirred to a stop. Through the window Quentin could see several people walking across the lawn toward him. Some of them wore army uniforms, and others were carrying cameras.

General Mainwaring opened the door of the helicopter and beckoned to Quentin. He helped Quentin and Flan down the steps of the helicopter. Then he saluted a man standing there surrounded by aides, army officers, reporters, and Secret Service men.

"Mr. President, may I introduce Mr. Quentin Stowe."

It was strange, Quentin thought, to see the leader of the whole country wearing a plain blue suit. He'd looked at a lot of pictures of kings and emperors in velvet robes and uniforms covered with gold braid and medals. The suit was better. Somehow it made Quentin feel more at ease.

"That thing on the boy's shoulder . . . the little green man . . . is called Flan," General Mainwaring explained nervously.

The President shook first Quentin's hand and then Flan's. "How do you do, Quentin . . . and Flan?" he said easily as the cameras clicked and reporters took notes. "Would you like to see the White House?"

Quentin looked back to where Momma was standing at the top of the helicopter steps. She waved for him to go along.

"Oh, yes, sir!" he said to the President.

As they walked toward the White House a dog ran out of some bushes. It began barking and growling at Flan. But the little man opened his mouth and howled like a raging wolf. The dog ran away with its tail between its legs.

The President laughed. "That's a good trick," he said. "I wish you'd teach it to me. I could use it sometimes when I speak to Congress."

"Look, George." As his parents caught up with Quentin, Mrs. Stowe pointed toward the porch. "It's the President's wife—the First Lady. Doesn't she look fine?"

The First Lady insisted on carrying Flan on her shoulder. From time to time the little man would whisper in her ear, and when he did, she laughed delightedly.

As they were about to enter the White House, a uniformed man with eagles on his shoulders ran up to the President. He whispered something, and the President whispered back. Quentin heard only a few words—"major crisis" and "armies gathering." But when the President turned around, he wasn't smiling anymore.

Still, he took them through the entire White House—even the places most visitors don't see.

123

There were the Library and the Map Room and the State Dining Room and rooms named for so many different colors that Quentin couldn't remember them all. In the East Room, all gold and white, Poppa looked up at the high ceiling in amazement. "It's bigger than my whole barn," he kept saying to himself.

Quentin most enjoyed seeing the Lincoln Bedroom. From here Abraham Lincoln himself had looked out at the first white stone blocks for the Washington Monument. Quentin wished Roselynn and Vincent were with him to see the President's home.

But then he remembered sadly how the money he'd given them had come back. Since then, neither Roselynn nor Vincent had spoken to him.

As they went back into the hall, a man in a gray suit rushed up and handed an envelope to the President. The President tore it open.

"Have the air force put on standby alert," he said to the messenger.

Then he spoke to Quentin. "I'm taking you to the Oval Office. I use it when I want to talk about big problems. And today we have a very big problem on our hands."

They entered the office, and the President sat at his huge desk. Mr. and Mrs. Stowe went to a couch, and Quentin sat in a soft chair with Flan squeezed in beside him.

"Quentin," the President began, "it seems you were telling the truth all the time, even if it was hard for us to believe. You really *do* have all the money in the world on your farm."

Quentin nodded slowly.

"I've had a lot of reports about the money," said the President. "But why don't you tell me yourself how you got it?"

Quentin told him the whole story.

"I see," said the President when he'd finished. "And now you can't wish the money away because you haven't got any wishes left."

"That's right, Mr. President."

"And General Mainwaring's men can't take it away because then you'd no longer have all the money in the world. Is that about the situation?"

"Yes . . . yes, sir."

"Well, at least you haven't broken any laws. If wishing were against the law, we'd all be in jail. But tell me something, Quentin."

"What?"

"If you had it all to do over again, would you still wish for all the money in the world?"

"Oh, no! No!" Quentin shook his head. "Our crops are all being squashed by the money, and I've had to haul water for the animals twice a day.

Roselynn Peabody and Vincent Arbor, my two best friends, won't even talk to me, and I can't even spend the money. It's just been one big problem for me ever since I got it."

The President frowned and stared at his desk for a long time. Finally he looked at Quentin again.

"The problem may be even bigger than you think," he said.

"I . . . I don't understand, sir."

"Quentin, all the people of all the countries of the world need things—things they must have money to buy. But you have all the money."

"But I can't help it. I'd give it all back if I could."

"Of course you would. But some countries don't understand that. They think the United States is keeping the money on purpose. And because of that, they say they're going to do something."

Mr. Stowe spoke up. "What are they going to do, Mr. President?"

The President's answer was just a whisper.

"War!"

"War!" cried Mrs. Stowe. "But you can't let that happen."

"There's very little I can do." The President looked at Quentin. "You have all the money. Nobody else has any."

He leaned wearily on the big desk. "People

who don't have anything," he said, "have nothing to lose. And when that happens, they sometimes fight. Just to feed themselves and their families . . . to stay alive. Even those who'd usually hate the idea of war."

"I understand," said Quentin. "I really do. But what can I do to make the money go back?"

"Flan?" said the President.

The little man peered over Quentin's arm. "Yes, your lordship?"

"Just call me Mr. President. I'm not a lord."

"Yes, Mr. President. What can I do for you?"

"Is there any way you can make the money go back where it belongs?"

"No. No, sir. The wishes are gone, and that's the end of it. It's the Law of the Leprechauns."

The President pushed a button on his desk. "Is there any way we could get that law changed?" he asked. "Just this once?"

"I never heard of that happening," said Flan.

"Who would I talk to about it?"

Flan scratched his head. "The Head Leprechaun, maybe. If you could find him. He lives in Ireland somewhere. But sometimes he looks like a leprechaun, and sometimes like an oak tree, and sometimes like a groundhog. He's very hard to find."

"The government of the United States ought to

be able to find a leprechaun," said the President. "Even the Head Leprechaun."

Just then the door of the office opened. A man entered, carrying a thick folder of papers under his arm.

"This is my Secretary of State," the President said.

He and the Secretary of State talked together in low voices. Then the Secretary of State picked up the telephone and made a call. Then a second call. And a third. Each one seemed to disturb him more than the last. Finally he whispered something into the President's ear. Quentin couldn't hear a word, but the look on the President's face got more and more worried.

Finally the President spoke to Quentin and Flan. "My Secretary of State tells me it's impossible to get a message to the Head Leprechaun," he said sadly. "Even the F.B.I. doesn't know how to locate leprechauns if they don't want to be found."

He looked squarely at the little man. "Flan, I now speak to you as the leader of this great country."

"What is it, Mr. President?"

"There has to be some way for Quentin to get more wishes. It's the only way we can end this money situation and avoid the chance of war.

Flan shook his head. "Quentin caught me and

made me say my name," he said. "That's the only time a leprechaun grants wishes. Except . . ."

Then he stopped talking. His face twisted itself into a strange half grin, half frown.

"Except when . . . what?" Quentin asked.

Everybody leaned forward, waiting for Flan's answer. But the little man just folded his arms and pressed his lips tightly together. It was clear he thought he'd said too much already.

Quentin looked first at his parents and then at the President. "There *is* a way to get more wishes," Quentin said. "Isn't there, Flan?"

The little man just stared at the floor for a long time. Then, still frowning, he gave a quick nod.

"I knew it! Tell us what it is," Quentin said to Flan.

This time the little man shook his head quickly from side to side.

"Why, Flan?" Quentin asked. "Why won't you tell us?"

"Because the Law of the Leprechauns won't allow me to," Flan snapped. "As it is, my punishment will be fearful if the Head Leprechaun discovers I've told you this much."

"I beg you, Flan," said the President. "For the good of the country."

"No," Flan replied firmly. "You must live by your laws, and I must live by mine."

For a long time nobody said anything. Then Poppa spoke. "If Flan won't talk, then there won't be any more wishes. You'll have to figure out some other way, Mr. President."

Suddenly the President looked very tired. "A lot of people think the President should have the answer to everything," he said. "I'd do anything to save the country from war. But this time I don't know what to do."

Mr. and Mrs. Stowe looked at one another in surprise. "You mean there isn't any answer?" Mrs. Stowe asked.

"None that I can think of. If there's an answer, you'll have to find it, Quentin. And you'll have to find it before another day goes by. Just remember, if a miracle happens and you get any more wishes, you must not ask for anything for yourself. Not even the ten-speed bike I'm told you want so much. You have to wish for the money to go back where it belongs. You have to!"

The whole world depending on him! On the jet plane returning to Cedar Ferry, Quentin tried to sleep.

But sleep was impossible. The whole world was waiting for him to do something.

But what?

# 11
# The Last of the Money

"Poppa?"

Quentin looked over at his father, who was at the steering wheel of their farm truck. Between them Flan was bouncing up and down on the seat.

"Yes, Quentin?"

"Do you really think another town meeting will do any good? Everybody got all mean and angry at the last one."

"I don't know, Quentin. The meeting won't be pleasant. But the people in town have a right to hear what the President said to you. They won't try to hurt you. I'll see to that."

There was a parking space just across from the Volunteer Fire Department. Just as before, Mayor Peabody was on the steps, greeting people as they entered.

"Money or no money, I've still got to watch over this rotten step," he said. "When the money starts moving again, we'll have it fixed."

Again the meeting was opened by Viola Trussker singing "The Star-Spangled Banner." Flan covered his ears with his hands and made terrible faces, especially when Mrs. Trussker swooped into the high notes at the middle of the song.

Finally Mayor Peabody tapped the speaker's table, and the hum of voices became quiet. "Quentin," said the mayor, "I'd like you and your father to come up here, please."

He looked over the tops of his glasses at Flan. "And bring the little green fellow along, too."

Quentin and his father took chairs. Flan sat on the table itself and crossed his legs.

"Now then," said the mayor. "A lot's happened in the last day or so. Quentin here has been to see the President. Quentin, why don't you tell all of us what he's going to do about the money?"

Slowly Quentin pushed back his chair and got to his feet. He could feel himself shaking. He gulped once.

"Nothing."

Mayor Peabody leaned forward. "What, Quentin? I didn't quite get that."

"I said the President can't do anything about the money," said Quentin in a voice that was too loud. "And he left the whole problem up to me, and now there's going to be a *war*!"

For a moment there was an awful silence. And then the people began shouting.

"We're never going to get our money back! And it's all his fault!"

"Weren't you listening? He said something about a war!"

"But if the President himself can't do anything . . ."

Mayor Peabody banged on the table, and the shouts quieted.

"Now let's just keep calm," said the mayor. "At our last meeting some folks got a little too upset, and I won't allow that to happen again. If anybody wants to say something, suppose you raise your hand."

Over in one corner, Walt Milleridge's hand shot up. Mayor Peabody pointed toward him. "Go ahead, Walt. Speak your piece."

"The way I understand it, Roscoe," said Milleridge, "it's not the Stowes that did this thing. It's that little green man. Is that right, Quentin?"

Quentin nodded.

"We've all known the Stowes for years," Mr. Milleridge went on. "They're good people, and I can't see that Quentin has done much that any other boy wouldn't do. Why don't we let them go back home so we can get on with the meeting?"

Several people agreed. Quentin got up and stretched out his hands to pick up Flan.

"Just a second!" shouted Mr. Milleridge. "Suppose you leave the green man right where he is. He's the cause of all this. He's the one we want to talk to."

Just as at the last meeting, the crowd was getting angrier by the minute. But this time they were angry at Flan.

As loud shouting filled the room, Quentin looked at his father. Mr. Stowe was walking away from the table.

"I don't want to leave Flan up here alone," said Quentin.

"I expect Flan can take care of himself." Mr. Stowe went to the back of the room. Quentin followed him. Flan stood on the tabletop, his hands on his hips.

"Now then," Milleridge went on. "You tell us, green man, why you can't just send all that money back where it came from."

"It's not in my power. Quentin caught me, and I gave him his three wishes. The bargain ends there."

"But Quentin doesn't want the money!" Emma Hobson shouted out. "Do you, Quentin?"

"No, ma'am," he answered.

"It makes no difference," said Flan. "I'm helpless too."

"Helpless," sneered Mr. Milleridge. "I'll say he's helpless." He pointed a finger at Flan. "Look at him. A little bit of a thing. Not only that, but he's like nobody else I ever saw. He's . . . he's *green*!"

"He's green!" someone else called out.

"He's green!"

The words became a chant that the people shouted over and over again. "He's green! He's green! He's green!"

The noise got louder and louder. But Flan just stood on the table, a smile on his face.

He lifted one tiny foot and tapped the toe of his shoe three times on the tabletop. Then he raised both arms over his head and brought them down sharply.

All at once the sound stopped. In the strange silence Quentin tried to look about the room.

But he could not. He couldn't move his head or his neck or even his eyes. He was frozen in place.

And so was everybody else in the room. Some were standing, and some were seated. Some had outstretched hands, and the arms of others were at their sides. But there was no movement. It was as if they had become a roomful of statues.

"Now then," said Flan, his eyes flashing. "I'll have my say. Yes, Quentin Stowe made a foolish wish. But today the rest of you are being even more foolish. Because of the way you've talked to me, I'm leaving Cedar Ferry. And with me goes even the slight chance of the money's being returned. So in the future, when you think of my green skin, think of that too. I can't help being green, just as Quentin Stowe couldn't help making a boy's wish. When you reach in your pockets for money and find only dust, remember—you brought it on yourselves!"

The little man hopped down from the table. He walked through the crowd of motionless people until he reached the door. Quentin heard him open it. Then there was a loud snap of his fingers.

"Hey, grab him! He's leaving."

"Yeah, don't let him get away!"

The people could move and speak again. The door slammed behind Flan, and for a moment nobody seemed sure of what to do.

*CR—RR—UNCH—CH!*

The sound came from outside. It was followed at once by Flan's high, angry voice.

"Curse your rotten steps anyway! I'm stuck!"

Mr. Stowe rushed to the door and threw it open. Quentin looked out and saw Flan.

At least he saw the top part of Flan. The little man had crashed down through the rotten place in the building's steps. But he had fallen through only as far as his waist. Now his top half stuck up through the wood, while underneath, his legs flopped about helplessly.

The people streamed out of the building. "Don't get near me!" Flan squeaked. "I'll change you all into caterpillars."

He continued to struggle. "Oh, curse the day I slept through my flying lesson. Woe is me!"

They made a big circle around the leprechaun. It wasn't hard to see that he was stuck fast. Without help, he'd never be able to free himself.

Both Quentin and Poppa stepped forward. Each held out a hand to the struggling leprechaun. He twisted away from Quentin and reached eagerly for Poppa's strong arm.

Then Quentin had an idea. "Poppa, get back!" he cried. "Don't let him take hold of you."

With a puzzled look on his face, Mr. Stowe did as he was told. Quentin knelt down beside the little man.

"You're stuck, aren't you, Flan?" he asked.

Flan's hands pressed against the step, trying to lift his body out of the hole. "Yes, lad," he said finally. "I guess I am."

"I could get you out."

Flan shook his head. "No, lad. I'd prefer aid from somebody else, thank you."

And then Quentin was sure. He knew Flan's secret!

"Nobody will help you, Flan. Not unless I tell them to."

For a long time Quentin and the little man stared at each other. Finally it was Flan who spoke. "You know, don't you, lad?"

"I think I do," said Quentin. "I already caught you and made you say your name. Now I must truly

138

rescue you from a fate worse than death, but then you'll have to grant me more wishes."

"That's nearly right" was the answer. "But there's a catch to it, and I might as well tell you, since you've guessed so much already. For you to get more wishes, I'd first have to *beg* you to rescue me. But since you made such a mess of your first wishes, I believe I'll just remain here—stuck in the steps forever. Anything, rather than plead for *your* help."

The little man turned up his nose and folded his arms across his chest. The talk was at an end.

Quentin looked about. He saw a face in the crowd. Yes, that would do it. That would have to do it.

"Mrs. Trussker," he called, "would you come over here?"

Viola Trussker jiggled her way to Quentin. She looked down at Flan. "Oh, he's so cute," she cooed. "Cute, cute, cute!"

Flan looked at Quentin in alarm. "You wouldn't," he pleaded. "You couldn't."

"Mrs. Trussker," said Quentin. "Flan likes your singing very much. Since he's stuck here, perhaps you could cheer him up with a song."

"No!" Flan cried. "No!"

"I'm a little afraid," said Mrs. Trussker. "I don't want him to turn me into a statue again."

"Flan can't do that spell now," said Quentin. "He has to tap his toe three times. And stuck in that hole, he hasn't got anything to tap against."

"Blast you!" Flan snarled. "That's the trouble with lads your age. You see far too much of what's going on around you."

"Well, if you're sure it's safe." Mrs. Trussker put a finger to her dimpled chin. "Now what will it be? Oh, I know so many songs. There's 'A Bicycle Built for Two' and 'I Love You Truly' and 'Silver Threads Among the Gold' and . . ."

"Oh, sing them all," said Quentin.

"Very well." Mrs. Trussker cleared her throat loudly.

*"Daisy, Daisy, give me your answer, do. . . ."*

"Oh, no," Flan moaned. "She sounds like a boat whistle, and she hasn't got one note right yet."

*"I'm half crazy, all for the love of yewww. . . ."*

"Quentin, it's cruel torture, that's what it is!"

*"It won't be a stylish marriage . . ."*

The singing, if you could call it that, was getting to be more than Quentin himself could stand. But he gritted his teeth. After all, the President of the United States was depending on him.

*"I can't afford a carriage . . ."*

"Enough!" Flan cried out. "My poor ears are hurting!"

*"But you'll look sweet . . ."*

"Will you give me three more wishes, Flan?"

"No."

*"Upon the seat . . ."*

"Will you give me two?"

Flan shook his head.

*"Of a bicycle built for twoooooooo. . . ."*

"Get her to stop, and release me from these steps," said Flan, "and I'll grant you one more wish. One! That's my final offer."

There was a loud cheer from people who were close enough to hear what Flan had said. Quentin asked Mrs. Trussker to stop. She pouted a bit, but at least the awful sound of her voice was stilled.

Quentin gripped Flan's arms. He pulled upward. At first nothing happened. And then with a splintering of wood Flan came up out of the hole in the steps like a cork from a bottle.

"I'm leaving here as fast as I can," the leprechaun announced. "Quick, lad. Your wish."

Quentin couldn't help thinking of all the wonderful things he could wish for himself. But he knew what the final wish had to be. He closed his eyes.

"I wish," he said slowly, "for all the money in the world to go back to where it came from. To where it really belongs."

"Don't forget to count, lad."

Quentin remembered his earlier wish. "One . . . two . . . three!"

He opened his eyes. The first thing he saw was Flan, running away down the street as fast as his legs could carry him.

And then he heard voices.

"It's money. Right here in my pocket."

"Real money. Listen to those coins jingle."

"Twenty-eight dollars and sixteen cents. And it's all mine."

Mr. Sedgewick's assistant came running up the street from the bank. "The money's back!" he cried. "Piles and piles of it!"

Quentin felt a tap on his shoulder. He turned around.

It was Mr. Milleridge. "I'm ashamed of the way I acted inside," he said. "I'd like you to have an ice-cream soda at my store. As a way of saying I'm sorry."

"Just so you know first that I can't pay for it," said Quentin. "You see, I didn't have any money in the first place."

He pushed his hands deep into his pockets. And to his surprise, he felt a coin. He pulled it out.

There was a picture of a king on the coin. But the king was smoking a pipe. And the crown on his head looked very much like a battered top hat.

"The soda will be free, Quentin. You deserve it."

Quentin was slurping the ice-cream soda when an army truck came speeding down the street outside. The driver was shouting something. Both Quentin and Mr. Milleridge listened.

"The money is gone from the fields! One second it was there, and the next it wasn't. It just disappeared!"

Mayor Peabody walked to the truck and spoke to the driver. The driver answered in a loud voice.

"Don't ask me how the money went away, and don't ask me where it went to. I just don't know."

Quentin couldn't help smiling.

# 12
# A Present from a Friend

Quentin sat cross-legged on his front porch, staring off into space. Momma was in the squeaky rocking chair, peeling apples.

"Flan's been gone a couple of days now," she said. "Do you miss him?"

"Well, he was somebody to play with," Quentin answered. "Especially after Roselynn and Vincent got mad at me."

"Oh, I expect they'll be along in a day or so," said Momma. "Sure, they were angry when they couldn't share any of the money. But deep down, they're good folks."

"Momma?"

"Yes, Quentin?"

"We always got along well with Mr. Milleridge and the Hobsons and all the other people in the village, didn't we?"

"Of course we did."

"Then why did they get so angry with me about the money? I didn't want to do anything to hurt them. But as soon as I got the money it was like everybody was just standing in line to hate me."

Momma sighed. "It'd take a wiser person than me to answer that," she said. "Money does strange things to people sometimes."

Poppa came around the corner of the house. There was a big grin on his face.

"Being under all that money didn't hurt the crops as much as I'd thought," he said. "It even protected some of the young plants from the hot sun. We'll have a harvest this year, in spite of everything. Looks like we'll be able to pay back what's owing with even a little left over. Won't that be fine, Ruth?"

"Don't count on that money until it's in your pocket," Momma replied. "Quentin, I've been meaning to ask you something."

"What?"

"Let's pretend you had your third wish all over again. What would it be?"

"Well . . ." Quentin thought about all the things he could wish for. Maybe a gold mine. Or a handful of diamonds. It seemed as if he should have gotten something for his three wishes.

"I could have asked Flan for . . ."

There was a distant rumbling sound. Quentin put a hand to his mouth. "You don't suppose . . ."

"That's just thunder," Poppa answered. "Thunder and heat lightning are normal for this time of year. Flan's gone forever, Quentin."

"Look." Momma pointed off down the road. "Somebody's coming."

"Looks like one of those army trucks," said Poppa. "I hope there won't be any more trouble."

The truck pulled up in front of the house. The driver shut off the motor and opened the door.

It was Sergeant Ray Tucker.

Quentin ran toward him. "Ray!" he cried out.

"Mind your manners, Quentin," said Momma. "You call a grown-up man 'Mister,' hear?"

"That's all right," said Ray. He put an arm around Quentin's shoulder. "We're pals. Right, Quentin?"

"Right," replied Quentin proudly.

"And I brought my pal a present," said Ray.

"You got a present for me?" Quentin looked Ray up and down. "Where is it?"

"Well, it's not really from me. It's from . . . Let's have a look."

Ray went to the rear of the truck and drew back the cloth. He reached inside and lifted out a new bike that sparkled in the sun.

"A ten-speed!" Quentin cried. "Is it for me, Ray?"

The sergeant nodded. Quentin ran his fingers over the blue frame, the glittering spokes, and the black-leather seat.

"The best that money can buy," said Ray. "And there's a card on the handlebars."

Carefully Quentin untied the ribbon around the card. The paper was smooth and white under his fingers.

He began to read.

*This is just my way of saying thank you for the fine thing you've done. The money is back, and the chance of war is over.*

*I'm not Flan, and I can't grant every wish you make. But I knew this was something you wanted. And I think you deserve to have it. Come and see me again soon.*

"Who's it from, Quentin?" Momma asked.

Without a word he handed her the note. At the

top, a picture of an eagle surrounded by a circle of stars had been pressed onto the paper. Below the eagle were the words:

## THE WHITE HOUSE

"My gracious!" Momma flopped back in her chair. "It's from the President!"

"He signed it himself, Momma. See? And look right there, where it says 'Your friend.'"

"I was ordered to bring it personally," said Ray. "And now I have to be going."

"Oh, Sergeant," said Momma. "Can't you stay for lunch?"

Ray shook his head. "But my camp is just a short distance from here," he said. "And I would like to come and taste some of those apples when you've baked 'em into pies."

"You just drop by anytime," said Momma. "I'll have some ready and waiting for you."

Ray hopped back into the truck. With a wave of his hand he rolled off down the road. He passed a boy and a girl who were riding bikes toward the house.

"Hi, Quentin!" called Vincent and Roselynn together.

They leaned their bikes against the big willow tree in the front yard. "We came to see if you wanted to go fishing," said Vincent.

"I don't know," Quentin replied. "All the pole I've got is that old willow stick."

"I brought an extra pole," said Roselynn. "With a reel and everything. You can use it if you want to."

"I'm still not sure . . ." Quentin began.

His mother grabbed him by an ear and pulled him close. "Quentin Stowe, those two are trying to make up for not being nice to you before," she whispered. "And you're not making it easy. Now you run along and be friends. Hear?"

"Hey, look at the new bike!" Vincent gave a low whistle and rubbed the blue frame. "Is that yours, Quentin?"

"It sure is," said Quentin proudly.

Roselynn looked at him sternly. "Quentin, when you sent that money back where it came from, did you keep out some for yourself?"

"Nope," said Quentin. "Not a cent."

"Then where did this new bike come from? It's the best one I ever saw."

Quentin looked toward Momma, who just winked at him.

"Oh, it's just a present."

Quentin got onto the bike and took the fishing pole that Roselynn held out to him.

"Just a present from a friend of mine."